CAPRICE

CAPRICE

·—•·•·•·•—·

COE BOOTH

SCHOLASTIC PRESS / NEW YORK

All rights reserved. Published by Scholastic Press, an imprint of Scholastic Inc.,
Publishers since 1920. SCHOLASTIC, SCHOLASTIC PRESS, and associated logos are
trademarks and/or registered trademarks of Scholastic Inc.

The publisher does not have any control over and does not assume any
responsibility for author or third-party websites or their content.

This book is a work of fiction. Names, characters, places, and incidents are
either the product of the author's imagination or are used fictitiously, and any
resemblance to actual persons, living or dead, business establishments,
events, or locales is entirely coincidental.

Library of Congress Cataloging-in-Publication Data available

ISBN 978-0-545-93334-6

10 9 8 7 6 5 4 3 2 1   22 23 24 25 26

Printed in the U.S.A. 37
First edition, May 2022

Book design by Elizabeth B. Parisi & Becky James

For Samantha

memories, part one

some memories are pictures,
flat and still.

some are videos,
little clips of life.

some memories are voices and music.
others are quiet, like holding your breath.

sometimes memories are blank spaces,
fuzzy question marks that punctuate time.

sometimes it's only your body that remembers
all the details nobody else knows.

• • • • •

I'm supposed to be packing, but I really can't get it together. Sitting on the floor, surrounded by all my clothes and books and *stuff*, all I can think is: Why does it have to end like this? My seven weeks here went by in something like five seconds, and if it wasn't for what happened last night, everything would have been perfect. But now, it's all over.

I need more time.

I shake my head and try to let go of all my feelings. I need to focus. Mom and Dad are gonna be here any minute and I know the first thing Mom is gonna say is, "Why aren't you packed? When we talked yesterday, I told you to make sure you were ready when we got here."

And Dad will say something like, "Saturday traffic is so unpredictable, Caprice. It can be almost as bad as weekdays, especially on Route 17."

It's a little after ten o'clock in the morning, and good thing they're late because I can use the extra time. It's hard to finish packing when I don't really wanna leave.

I fold my T-shirts into perfect little rectangles. Too perfect. But all the folding and perfecting keeps me from thinking about anything else, keeps me from slipping into my feelings.

It keeps me from thinking about last night and how I messed everything up.

All of a sudden I'm hit with a wave of heavy sadness again.

"You okay?" my roommate Terra asks with that cute New Zealand accent I'm really gonna miss.

I glance up at her just long enough to see the worry in her eyes.

Then I look away. "Um, I'm sorry I ruined your last night. I didn't mean to—"

"It's not *my* last night, silly. I'll be back in a week." She sits on the floor next to me.

"You know what I mean. I made you leave the party early and—"

"Caprice, I just want you to be alright," she says. "I mean, last night I . . ." She shakes her head. "I'm sorry. I didn't know what to do."

"You did everything right," I say. "Seriously."

The truth is, I still don't know why I fell apart. It was scary. It's still scary. I used to be able to keep all of it inside, but now, I don't know. Maybe I can't anymore.

"Do you wanna talk to your parents about it? I mean, maybe they—"

"No way!" The words tumble out of my mouth. "Can we just act like everything's normal?"

"No problem." She gives me a weak half smile. "Nothing happened."

I breathe out and smile back. "Thanks."

I lean over and give Terra a hug. All I have to do is try to let all those feelings go. My parents will be here any minute.

When I talked to Mom yesterday, she got another call in the middle of our conversation. It was someone calling from Baltimore, so she had to go. Probably something about Grandma.

After we hung up, I don't know. It was hard to get in the mood for the party. Like, I hadn't heard Mom mention Grandma in forever, and now, outta nowhere, she was getting a phone call about her. It kinda made me wonder what was going on, if Grandma was okay.

I still don't know. But I try to push that out of my mind, too.

I stand up and look around the room one last time. Terra's side is lavender and gray and overloaded with books. My side looks like I was never here.

It's gonna be harder leaving Ainsley International School than I ever thought it would be. It's hard to explain, but I feel it. This seven-week Summer Leadership Program, and just *being* here, has changed me. On the outside, I know I'm still me, the same girl from Newark I was when I got here. But inside, I can feel it. I'm different.

I grab my phone off the desk and text Mom.

> are u here

No answer.

"I wish you could stay," Terra says quietly. "Like, for good."

"Me too."

She gets up from the floor and moves over to her bed. "You're the best roommate I've had, and I've been here since fifth grade."

All I can do is smile.

"Did you see Ms. Adams dancing last night?" Terra asks, laughing. "What *was* that?"

I laugh with her. "Maybe that's the way they danced back in the eighties or something."

"Or like the seventies!"

"She's not *that* old," I say. "She's just kinda . . . *stiff*."

We burst out laughing even louder. I need this. I need to remember the fun things about the party.

Finally, I get a text back from Mom.

> The head of school asked to meet with us. Be there after.

I suck in my breath. "Dr. Suzanne wants to meet with my parents," I tell Terra. "Do you think she knows what happened?"

"No way. I'm the only one."

"Then what does she wanna talk to them about?"

Terra shrugs. "Let's wait and find out."

I sit down at my desk and remind myself to breathe. The meeting probably has nothing to do with last night. I'm just being paranoid.

A minute later I get another text, this time from Nicole.

what time are you getting here already

It's only her sixth or seventh text of the morning, which is pretty good for her. I don't wanna tell her about Mom and Dad's meeting with the head of school, not until I know what it's about, so I just text back:

mom and dad are late picking me up 😣

god i cant wait anymore!!!

i'll text u when we're on the way home

come straight to the center & get me

☺☺

Seven weeks away hasn't been easy. Not for either of us. I miss her so bad, and I know she misses me, too. Since I've been here, me and her texted all the time, but there's hardly been time for anything else. I hadn't actually heard Nicole's voice since my first week here.

Terra takes her blanket and sheets off her bed. "I was hoping our parents would get to meet each other," she says. "But my mum only left D.C. about two hours ago."

My parents would like Terra's mom. I got to meet her already, my third week at Ainsley. She came up to talk to the Leadership Program about careers in diplomacy, which I didn't even know was a thing. Terra's mom is pretty famous in New Zealand. She won two gold medals in the Olympics for diving before Terra was born. The way she described her job—all of the traveling, meeting world leaders, trying to keep countries from going to war—sounded so cool. Terra said it *is* cool, but her mom is busy 24/7. It's definitely not something Terra would ever do for her career.

Me? I still don't know what I wanna do, and if this Summer Leadership Program was supposed to help with that, it didn't work. It just showed me that there are, like, a billion different careers out there.

"They still might meet," I say, standing up and helping Terra get the dirty sheets into her giant polka-dot laundry bag. "Depending on how long Dr. Suzanne keeps my parents in her office."

"True."

While we wait, I help Terra put clean sheets on her bed and straighten up the room so it'll look nice when she gets back from vacation.

At least she gets to come back.

I go down the hall to the supplies closet where they have brooms and dustpans. On the way, I pass Deja's empty room. She had to leave early to catch her flight home. After the party, I was supposed to meet her at the lake, where a lot of kids were hanging out. But I never made it there.

When I first came to Ainsley, I was kinda worried I was gonna be the only Black girl here, but there were three of us: Deja, Kimberly, and me. The only difference is, they're Ainsley students all year round. Deja took Kimberly home with her to Toronto for the break. Kimberly is from Ghana, way too far to go home for just a week. I wish I'd gotten a chance to say goodbye.

Terra is sorting through her books when I get back. On top, she has this book that's required reading for the eighth graders. But instead of reading that, she's flipping through her Grand Canyon travel guide for the thousandth time.

"You excited about your trip?" I ask her.

"Can't wait!" she says. "My mum and I are on a mission to hike in every state in America, but the Grand Canyon is going to be the best."

Terra's already been to Montana, Texas, Maine, Oregon, and Hawaii. Places I've never been to and I'm *from* this country. Kinda embarrassing.

"What about you?" she asks me. "Going anywhere before summer's over?"

It's so funny, but I never even think about going anywhere. I can't even remember the last trip my family went on.

"No, I don't think so," I say. "My friends spend most of the summer at, like, our community center."

"Oh," she says. "That sounds like fun."

"It is," I say fast. "I missed most of everything, but it's okay there. Fun."

I need to stop rambling, so I begin sweeping my side of the room, under my desk and bed. Then I do the same for Terra's side while she finishes getting packed. It doesn't take long for our room to start looking pretty decent. *Our* room. It's weird how soon I started feeling at home here, and now it's over.

I look up and see Mom and Dad standing in the doorway.

"You're here!" I shout, and drop the broom. "What did Dr. Suzanne want? Tell me, tell me."

Dad clears his throat. "That the way you greet us after a whole summer away?"

Mom comes into the room and wraps her arms around me. It feels *so* good. "My baby," she says. "I missed you so much."

Dad's hug is next. He brushes a loose loc from my face and kisses my forehead. Mom rubs my back. They're both here. Together.

Yeah, they both drove me up to Ainsley at the start of the summer, but they hardly talked, and when they did it was only about the traffic or where we were gonna stop for lunch. Stuff like that. The three-and-a-half-hour car ride from Newark to upstate New York felt like two days.

While I've been at Ainsley, Mom went to Detroit to work with Dad and see if they were gonna get back together or stay separated. I can tell right away things between them are different. *Better.* Both of them are hugging me and smiling, and it's like we're a family again. Maybe they worked out whatever problems they had. Hopefully.

Dad says hi to Terra, and of course Mom hugs her. Then Mom sits down on my bed while Dad zips up my suitcase.

"Okay, I'll end the suspense," Mom says. She's excited and kinda bouncy. "Dr. Suzanne called us yesterday and asked to meet with us before we picked you up. When we got here, she told us all about how impressed she's been with you this summer."

"She was?"

"She *is.*"

Impressed. I've been hearing that word a lot lately, ever since I decided to get serious about school and everything else. I mean, I've always done well in school, but in seventh grade I turned things up. Way up. All my teachers in Newark were *impressed*, too.

"What did she say?" I hold my breath waiting for Mom to tell me what's going on.

"Dr. Suzanne told us about everything you did this summer, how well you fit in with the Ainsley girls, and how she believes this is a school you will blossom in."

Me and Terra look at each other, and she lets out a little squeal.

"And because of all that," Dad continues, "Dr. Suzanne asked your mom and me if we would be interested in having you attend Ainsley during the school year."

Now Terra's smile grows so large, she has to hide her happiness with her hands.

"What does that mean?" I ask Mom. It's like I need to hear the words.

"Dr. Suzanne is inviting you to become a student here, tuition-free. Your dad and I will have to cover part of your room fees, but everything else will be taken care of by a scholarship."

Finally, Terra can't hold it in anymore. She starts giggling out loud.

That gets me giggling, too. "For the whole year?"

"Not just this year," Mom says. "She said you can stay through high school, too. It's all such an incredibly generous offer, something we could never afford otherwise. I mean, this school is expensive!"

"But—" In that moment, it feels like reality is starting to sink in, but I want everything to slow down. I need to think everything through. I mean, if I accept Dr. Suzanne's offer, that would mean I'll do eighth grade at Ainsley.

And not in Newark with Nicole.

"We told her we were sure you would jump at this opportunity," Mom says.

Dad adds, "Because you been talking our ears off about how great this place is."

"Right!" Mom says. "Dr. Suzanne gave us this whole packet of information and forms and everything, but she wants you to call her sometime next week. I think she wants to make sure you haven't changed your mind about coming."

Changed my *mind*?

"But—" I start, before realizing I don't know what to say.

"I'm so happy," Terra says, and the next thing I know we're hugging and shrieking and jumping up and down. Even Mom and Dad have to laugh at us.

I know, there's still a lot to think about. But right now, I decide to just be happy.

I mean, this could be the second chance I wanted.

If I decide to come back.

Driving back into Newark after so many hours in the car, it feels like I've been away for a long, long time. Seeing all the people out shopping on Ferry Street, hearing all the different kinds of music pumping from people's cars, and smelling the thick spices when Dad stops the car at a red light right next to the halal food truck that's always out in front of the electronics store. Everything is the same. Noisy and colorful and alive.

I missed all of this.

The drive home was completely opposite from the drive up to Ainsley. This time Mom and Dad were actually talking with each other, even joking around when some of those old R&B songs came on the radio from *back in the day*. It felt the way it did before Dad started going away for his job, before everything changed.

And yeah, they talked business, too. They *always* do. But they weren't arguing. It felt like they were partners again.

I was talking a lot, too, telling Mom and Dad *everything* about Ainsley. Everything except what happened last night. I told them about all the projects and activities, how I started to learn how to play lacrosse, which I'd never even heard of before, and how much I loved hanging out by the pond with the other girls after dinner, especially when this girl Erin would play her guitar and sing.

The one thing I haven't talked about is Grandma and what the phone call was about yesterday. Mom doesn't bring it up either.

"Don't forget," I say. "Drop me off at the Center."

Dad shakes his head. "That's probably—what?—the fourth time you've said that? Fifth?"

"At least," Mom says. "We get it. You're anxious to get back to the Center, like that place is going somewhere."

"It's not the Center," I say. "It's Nicole!" I start to feel the excitement in my stomach again. We've never been apart from each other this long before.

Dad turns the corner and we drive down Chambers Street. He could have turned anywhere, but he had to go the way that passes our house. Our *old* house. As it comes into view, I see the short hedges around the little yard and the driveway that's lined with colorful stones that Mom and I painted. I loved those stones. I don't know why we didn't take them with us.

I look away, to the other side of the block, as we pass Mrs. Scott's house with the yellow lace curtains, and Ms. Bailey's house with the red awnings. I can't stand that we don't still live here, that we couldn't afford to anymore. It feels like my family's epic failure. And it hurts.

We're all quiet as we drive by. And for the next block, too. Then Dad pulls up in front of the Center. "Here you go, kiddo," he says.

I open the door and hop out. "See you in a few." I wave goodbye to them.

Dad doesn't drive off, and I know he's waiting to see me go inside, so I walk up the path to the Center, something I've done a million and one times. Only now it feels the same *and* different. This place has always been like my second home. If you count summers, I'm here *more* than school.

But now, after seven weeks away, it feels like I'm new here. All of a sudden, I don't know what to expect. I pull open the large glass door and I'm blasted by the air-conditioning. And the noise.

Saturdays are always kinda busy at the Center. There are sports teams playing in the gym or on the field out back. There are programs for everyone, not just kids. The new mom group meets on Saturdays and the senior citizens have bus rides to the casinos and outlet malls. When I step inside, it's people everywhere, all doing different things. I have to laugh.

I check the schedule board to see where Nicole would be right now. Dance class. Of course.

I run down the hall to the rehearsal room and peek in through a little gap in the shade that's covering the window on the door. All the girls are in the middle of an African dance routine, working hard. Arms are flying and bare feet are bouncing off the ground, all to the rhythm of drums from the speakers. Nicole is in the front row, moving gracefully, happy. I love seeing her like that.

Abeni, our dance teacher, is in front of the room counting out the beats and calling out the steps. "C'mon, people," she says. "The festival is a week away. You want to look like this?"

I keep watching, smiling, wishing I could have been a part of this dance. There's so much energy. While I'm watching, I see Nicole turn left while everyone else turns right. She laughs and dances in place for a few beats and then turns to the left again, this time with everyone else. I wouldn't have known it was a mistake if she hadn't laughed.

I let out a little giggle, then I have to move away from the door so nobody can see me. I don't wanna distract Nicole. I just wanna surprise her when she's finished.

So I stand there and wait with my back pressed up against the wall. Kids run up and down the hall, wearing karate gis or carrying tennis rackets or skateboards. My favorite little girl, Miriam, carrying a Ziploc bag of colored beads, stops running down the hall when she sees me and gives me a hug. "I thought you were never coming back," she says, her arms around my waist.

"I told you I was." I lean over and press my cheek against hers. "How's your summer? Having fun?"

"Tons," she says. "I'm late for jewelry class." She takes off running down the hall and yells, "Don't go away again!"

I laugh. Miriam was my second-grade buddy last year, someone I looked out for. Of course, this year, she'll be my third-grade buddy. *If* I stay in Newark. *If* I don't take Dr. Suzanne's offer.

But I'm not gonna think about any of that now. I'm back in Newark, back at the Center, back with my best friend. And that's what I'm gonna concentrate on. Being here. Not there.

Finally, I hear, "Caprice! You're back!"

Nicole runs to me and grabs me so hard, all I can do is laugh and say, "You're hurting me!" But the truth is, I love it. It feels good being missed.

"Did you see the dance? It's gonna be amazing this year."

"Yeah, it looks good!"

"I have news!" Nicole says with a huge smile on her face. She grabs my hand and pulls me down the hall, away from everybody else who's coming outta the rehearsal room.

We turn the corner and run toward the double doors at that end of the hall, decorated with cutouts of tulips and windmills. We look over our shoulders and then slip through the doors. Yeah, we know we're not supposed to be in the preschool part of the Center, but that's never stopped us before.

This place used to be *ours*.

We run to our old classroom, room 6, and duck inside. All the little chairs are on top of the tiny desks. It's hard to believe we were ever that small.

"What's the news?" I ask, even though I can already guess. Only one thing makes Nicole's eyes light up like this. "Who is he?" I whisper.

"How did you know?"

"I know *you*!"

Nicole sighs like I'm blowing her big surprise. "Okay, okay," she says. "You guessed it. I have a *boyfriend*!" Nicole smiles so big it looks like her face might break.

"A boyfriend? Why didn't you tell me? Who is he?"

"You don't know him." She giggles. "His name is Anthony. He's only here for the summer, but we're trying to get his mother to let him stay in Newark forever. He's staying with his uncle. He's the guy who owns the pizza shop."

"Mr. Polazzo?"

"Yeah. Anthony is helping him out at the shop *and* he's on the baseball team. He's a pitcher. Really good, too. He has a killer curveball."

I was only gone seven weeks and now Nicole knows everything about baseball. Weird.

I don't know what to say. Nicole spent all of seventh grade in boyfriend-getting mode. She talked to a couple boys, but nothing really worked out. Personally, I never understood the whole *obsession*. To me, if it happens, it happens. But for Nicole, this is what she's been wanting for a long time.

I wrap my arms around her and give her a big hug. "Is he *the one*?"

She nods. "I think so. He's so sweet and cute and just, I don't know, like, perfect."

"I can't wait to meet Mr. Perfect," I tell her.

"I mean, he's not *really* perfect. He's just perfect for me."

"Awwwww."

Nicole covers her face. "Stop!"

Nicole and I stay in our old pre-K classroom catching up on all the drama I missed being away from the Center. Basically, it's all the same stuff with different people, but still, I need to know!

"Now that you're back," Nicole says, "we need to start shopping for school. We have to be cute this year because we're gonna be running things now. Finally!"

"Running things?"

"They're having a big sale at Sephora," she says. "There's nothing wrong with wearing a little makeup, Caprice. We're gonna be in eighth grade."

Now I *know* I'm back. Only thing, it feels like we're having the exact same conversation we had right before I left.

As Nicole goes on and on about eighth grade and how great it's gonna be, especially when we have the right clothes and makeup, I sit there and listen. She's my best friend and I love how excited she gets about all of these things, even though I could care less.

All the while she talks, part of me feels terrible. Like, kinda guilty. How am I gonna tell her about the offer from Ainsley? *Should* I even tell her at all? I mean, I haven't made my decision yet, so maybe I shouldn't even bring it up.

Still, I feel bad not telling her. I don't like keeping secrets from Nicole. Especially one this big.

—•—•—•—

"Why are we going this way?" Nicole asks when I turn the corner by the hardware store instead of going straight.

I just can't go by my old house twice in one day.

"Oh, I know," she says, and I'm waiting to hear what she's gonna say. "Zebra Cakes!"

I giggle, relieved. "Exactly. I couldn't find them anywhere near Ainsley. Those people don't know what they're missing!"

We go to the candy store, and when Mr. Brownlee sees me he's all like, "Caprice. You're back. Thought you forgot 'bout us 'round here."

"Never!" I say, and me and him fist-bump. Mr. Brownlee is cool. He's like my dad's age, but he tries to act young.

"Don't leave us no more."

"Don't worry," Nicole says, slipping her arm around my waist. "I'm not letting her go again."

"Better not." Mr. Brownlee waves his finger at her.

I head straight for the Little Debbie rack. "Yes!"

Just holding that little black-and-white cake in my hands makes my mouth water. The truth is, I didn't even think about Zebra Cakes once while I was away and I wasn't thinking about them today, but now that Nicole's mentioned them, I'm due to have one.

I wanna eat it on the way to my place, but Nicole says, "Don't do it. Trust me."

"Why?"

"My lips are sealed."

"Oh, I get it!"

Nicole laughs.

Her mom owns a bakery/cafe on Market Street. I bet she brought something back for me. Something much better than a Zebra Cake.

"Ooh," I say, "I can't wait!" It feels so good to walk in my neighborhood with my best friend again.

As we get closer to my house, I feel myself start to sink. Not that it's bad. It's not. It's an okay two-family house on the corner with huge flowerpots next to the outside steps. We're on the top floor. The only thing is, all the time I was away, I kept imagining coming home to the other house.

My home.

Me and Nicole walk up the steps, and I know something's wrong the second we step inside. Dad's at the table in the little kitchen. His laptop is open in front of him, the way it always is, but he isn't even staring at it. He's too busy looking up at Mom, who's leaning against the counter, talking on her phone.

I've only seen Dad in this apartment a couple times since we moved here in the spring, and it feels strange seeing him now in the tiny kitchen that belongs to just me and Mom. It's like he's too big for this place.

Mom called it downsizing, moving here. She and Dad had to downsize everything since the business was struggling, and she thought the house was too big for just the two of us. Moving to a smaller place saved us a lot of money. And she said we could always move into another house when Dad came back.

If he comes back.

But he's here now. So that's something.

Without even hearing what Mom's saying, I know it has to be about Grandma. I try to read Mom's face, to figure out how bad things are, but all I'm getting is a worried look. And maybe a little anger.

"I don't understand why it took so long," she tells the person on the other end of the phone. "I mean, when are you going to have some answers?"

The weird thing is, I haven't seen Grandma since I was a little kid, since we moved away from Baltimore. We used to live with her, but we don't talk to her or any of Mom's family anymore. It's like there's this big dividing line. Grandma's on one side with all my aunts, uncles, and cousins. And Mom's on the other side with just me and Dad.

Dad gets up and gives Nicole a hug. I smile watching them, even though I still kinda feel guilty. Like, why do I still have a dad when she doesn't? Dad asks Nicole how everything's going and how her mom and brothers are, and while they talk, I watch Mom. Her face is tight, hard to read. "Is Grandma alright?" I whisper to Dad.

He gives a head shake. "I don't know, but something's going on." He goes over to Mom, and then he does something I haven't seen in a long time. He grabs hold of her hand and doesn't let go.

"I'm not sure," Mom says into the phone. "The last time I saw her, she was in good health. I mean, she was overweight, and she had to use one of those sleep machines to help her breathe . . . Yeah, that. But . . ." Mom looks completely lost as she listens to whoever she's talking to. "Um, she's only sixty-one—no, sixty-three. She's sixty-three."

Dad rubs Mom's hand.

"No, uh, I don't know the name of her regular doctor," Mom says. "I can try to find out."

Next to me, Nicole whispers, "Who's sick?"

"My grandmother, I think. In Baltimore."

We wait for a little while longer, still not getting too much information from Mom's side of the conversation.

"Why don't you get your stuff together?" Dad whispers to me, still holding Mom's hand. "I'll drop you girls off at Nicole's."

"But . . ." I wanna know what's happening.

"Let your mom talk," he says. "She'll fill you in later."

I stand there for a few more seconds, then me and Nicole go down the hall to my room, which is in the back, right over the backyard. My so-called room is tiny, and the ceiling is slanted so there's only one small round window. There's just enough room for my bed and dresser and that's about it. I used to have a desk and a huge bookcase with a ton of books, but all of that's in some storage place by the highway.

Nicole closes my bedroom door behind us. "What do you think is going on with your grandmother?" she asks in a kind of loud whisper, even though nobody else is anywhere near us.

I shrug.

"You don't think she . . . ?"

"No, no," I say real fast. "I don't think so. I mean, my mom would probably be crying or something, even though we really aren't that close to her. I mean, we haven't seen her in forever."

"Why not?"

I shrug again. "Like, family drama and stuff." I definitely know more, but I don't wanna get into it with Nicole. Anyway, all that stuff happened a billion years ago.

I get down on the floor and open my suitcase. Here I am packing again when I haven't even unpacked yet. I don't know if I'm coming or going.

Everything in my suitcase is mixed up. I pull clothes out and try to make two piles: clean and dirty, but I can't tell one from the other. Finally, I find some pajama pants that aren't too dirty, and a clean T-shirt and jeans to wear tomorrow. I roll everything up and shove it in my backpack.

"You don't have shorts?" Nicole asks. "Don't you want to show your legs *ever*?"

"Who am I showing my legs to?"

"Boys. Who else?"

"Well, they can use their imagination," I tell her.

Nicole reaches into my suitcase. "What about these?" She holds up one of my many Ainsley Angels shorts. I practically lived in them while I was there. "They're kind of basic," she says, "but I guess you can wear these to the game."

I forgot we were going to the baseball game tomorrow.

"Sooo," Nicole says. The way her voice changes, I know what she's gonna ask me. "Meet any cute boys up there?"

I take the shorts from her and throw them in my dirty pile. "You remember Ainsley is all-girls, right?"

"I know, but don't they have, like, a boys' school across the lake or something? That's the way it is in the movies."

I shake my head. I could tell her about the party last night, where boys *did* come from Kentworth Academy, the all-boys school that is *not* on the other side of the lake, but I don't wanna open up that conversation.

"You still writing?" Nicole asks, flipping through a notebook I stuck in one of the pockets inside my suitcase. She reads, "'Memories, part one. Some memories are pictures, flat and—'"

"No! Don't read that one. I'm still working on it."

"Why can't your sad poems rhyme?"

"They're not really poems. Or sad. They're just thoughts. *Deep thoughts*." I force myself to laugh a little. "And they're *private*." I snatch the book outta her hands and slip it into my backpack. I'll share most of them with her, but I need to be the one who decides which ones and when.

Nicole shrugs and says, "I can't wait for you to meet Anthony. I told him so much about you."

"That's funny because you didn't tell me *anything* about him. I mean, you could have texted me or something."

"I wanted to tell you in person, like, face-to-face. Anthony is too important for texting."

"Oh man, Nicole. You sound like you're in lovvve!"

"Stop it!" She picks up a sock from my dirty pile and throws it at my face. It hits me right in my open mouth.

"Ewww," I scream, and try to wipe the sock dirt off my tongue.

"Sorry, sorry!" Nicole doubles over, laughing.

I laugh, too. "I couldn't wait to get home and this is how you treat me?"

"Sorry!" she says again.

That's when Mom sticks her head in the doorway. "You girls ready?"

"Almost." I throw some underwear and my satin bonnet in the backpack, then search through my suitcase for the pouch where I keep all my girl stuff.

"Hurry up," Mom says. "Your dad wants to get a run in after he drops you off."

I find the pouch and stick it in a pocket of my backpack. "Ready," I say. "But, Mom, is Grandma gonna be alright?"

Mom sighs heavily. "We're not sure yet. There was an incident last night. Her pastor visited and found her almost unconscious. That's when they called me."

"When we were on the phone?"

"Yeah. He said she was pretty out of it, so he called 911 and the ambulance took her to the hospital."

"Is it bad?"

"Well, nobody knows yet. The doctors are running tests, so we have to wait."

"Should I stay home and—?"

"No, no. Don't worry, baby. She's in the hospital, safe. Try to have fun tonight." She kisses me on the forehead. "C'mon, your dad's in a rush."

As usual.

"And remember," Mom says, "tomorrow's your dad's last night home."

Just like the last time he came home, Dad can only stay for the weekend. He has to get back to Detroit, back to work. There's never enough time with him.

"I'll come back early," I tell her.

Next to me Nicole loud-whispers, "The baseball game."

"What baseball game?" Mom asks.

Nicole looks up at her, like she's surprised Mom heard her.

"Me and Nicole wanna go see the game tomorrow. I'll come home right after it's done."

"Okay, be good. And thank Mrs. Valentine for having you over."

"I will." I throw the backpack over one shoulder. "I hope Grandma's gonna be okay," I say.

Mom wraps her arms around me, and I can feel her slip something into my back pocket. "Me too."

＊＊＊＊＊

As soon as I step into Nicole's house, her mom is there waiting for me. "Look at you," she says, grabbing me in a hug. "Miss World Traveler!"

"Well, not really," I mumble into the hug. "I was just upstate, in New York."

"Same difference," she says, finally letting go of me. "Come into the kitchen. I have a surprise for you."

Yes!

To welcome me back, Mrs. Valentine has brought home some goodies from the bakery. She puts the box down on the table and opens it.

"Cannolis!" I practically shout.

She smiles. "I knew you'd be happy. You better grab what you want now before those boys see that box."

I reach in and take one that is practically bursting with filling. I bite into it, and the sweet creamy cheese and crispy crunch are so good. I eat the whole thing before I thank Mrs. Valentine. "I missed these so much," I tell her.

Nicole's twin brothers come out of their room with their backpacks. Trevor is also carrying his basketball. They're sixteen, tall, and always hungry. And just like Mrs. Valentine predicted, they spot the bakery box right away and attack the cannolis like wolves. "Dad's outside," Vincent says, munching away.

Trevor shoves a cannoli in his mouth, whole. "See ya tomorrow, Ma," he says with a full mouth. He grabs another one on his way out.

"Give your dad trouble," Mrs. Valentine calls after them as they leave. Under her breath, she adds, "Why should my ex have it so easy?"

I laugh. Then I look in the box, hoping they left something behind. Nope. It's empty.

Trevor and Vincent go to their dad's house every other weekend. I always sleep over at Nicole's house on the weekends they're away. Then she comes to my house the other weekend. After Nicole's dad died when we were in fourth grade, I didn't want her to feel alone when her brothers were away. And I didn't want her to feel bad that they still had a dad when she didn't. Since then, we've never missed a sleepover. Except for this summer.

Me, Nicole, and Mrs. Valentine hang out for awhile. We order pizza, Caesar salad, and garlic knots, and when it comes, all three of us eat and laugh and eat some more. "Okay, this is the last story," Mrs. Valentine says, laughing even before she tells us. "This woman comes into the bakery with her daughter who's like four. They don't want to buy anything. Guess what they want?"

Me and Nicole look at each other. "What?" Nicole asks.

Mrs. Valentine laughs again. "The woman goes, 'This is a serious question. How much would it cost for my daughter to go back there, into the kitchen, and lick the spoons?'"

I laugh. "Actually, that would be pretty awesome!"

"All those different kinds of batter," Nicole says. Her eyes light up. "Can *I* do that, Mom?"

"No!"

We're all laughing.

By the time I get to Nicole's room, I'm stuffed and happy. "Your mom is hilarious," I say, flopping down on Nicole's bed. I'm too full to move. "I missed good pizza so much. And this bed!"

Everything about Nicole's room is the same, but for some reason, it looks brighter than normal. More sparkly.

"Check this out." Nicole holds open a big makeup palette. "Do you watch Diva Quilana's beauty channel?" She doesn't wait for me to answer no. "This is her first official palette. Cool, right?"

The colors are pretty and very summery. Lots of light pinks and mauves and orchids. They would look nice on Nicole. *Everything* looks nice on Nicole.

"Quilana has lip gloss, too," she says. "My mom let me buy a lot of her stuff. I'm gonna use it for the festival. And my party. It was so expensive, Mom told me never to ask for makeup again!" She laughs. "Anthony doesn't really like girls that wear a lot of makeup. He says I'm prettier without it."

"Awwww," I say, giggling. "Your *boyfriend* thinks you're sooo pretty!"

"Caprice, you can't keep doing this!" Nicole is loving it though.

"Try and stop me!"

We laugh for a little longer, me making kissing noises, her trying to act like it's bothering her. She's been wanting a boyfriend for over a year, so I have to be happy for her.

Finally, she says, "Come on, let me give you a makeover."

"I'm good," I say.

"You're more than good. But just for fun."

Before I know it, I'm sitting still as Nicole paints my face, adding color to my cheeks and lips, and trying out the different eye shadows. "Lilac is your signature shade," she tells me, sounding more like one of those makeup video girls than Nicole. "You should buy a lilac dress for my party."

She's looking right into my eyes, brushing the soft powder across my lid. It's hard to look away. But I do. I can't tell her that

I might not be here for her party. How can I tell her that?

When my face is done, she looks at my hair. "I thought you were gonna start wearing your hair out, Caprice. You can't look like a little girl forever." She lets my locs out of the ponytail I always have them in. They look bad, all dry and frizzy from all the swimming I did at Ainsley. Nicole runs her fingers through them, fanning them out over my shoulders. "See? You look like a teenager now."

Sitting there, letting Nicole make me over, it's hard not to think of how many times we've done this. Nicole, happily painting me, changing me. Me, just letting her do it.

In the mirror with my hair out and my face full of color, I don't look like myself. I look fancy, the kinda girl boys would probably look at. I gather all my locs together. "I'm not a teenager."

"In three months you will be. Well, three and a half. Exactly two months after me."

Me and Nicole were both born on the eleventh, her in October and me in December. Still, it's kinda annoying how she always finds ways to remind me she's older than me. I slip the elastic band back on my hair, making me look slightly more like myself. "I'll start wearing it out in three and a half months, then."

"Well, can you at least wear it out for my party?"

I nod. "Okay, I'll do that. For you."

She claps. "Yes! I'm so happy you're back. You can help me plan the party and pick out my dress. I saw some nice dresses at that new store next to Burger King. Let's go tomorrow before the baseball game. Just to look."

She's talking so fast, and I get it. She's excited. It's like she's trying to catch up on everything we haven't done this summer, all at once.

Meanwhile, I'm not even telling her about *my* summer.

"Oh yeah." Nicole jumps up. "You have to see what we're gonna wear for the dance at the festival. Abeni says this material is from Nigeria." She goes to her overstuffed closet and pulls out a beautiful blue dress with a gold-and-red design around the neckline.

I go over to feel the material. "Wow."

"I know, right? Gina's dress is even prettier than ours, but I still love this."

"Did you try to get the lead?" I ask, trying to keep my voice soft. I don't want Nicole to feel bad.

She shrugs. "Abeni knew I wanted it." She looks down for a second, then says, "Why keep auditioning when Gina's her favorite? Anyway, I really wanna spend more time singing. My voice is—I don't know. Like, maybe it could be okay, decent, if I work at it, you know? It's like I'm always doing so many other things."

I nod. "Yeah, you have a good voice."

"I just want to . . . Forget it. I'm just, it's not that serious, right? I mean, I have a solo in the dance. That's good enough. And if I got the lead, I wouldn't have that much time to spend with Anthony, so . . ."

I try to push aside everything she just said and focus on Anthony, because I know that's what's important to her right now. He's the one she's thinking about. But I wish we could talk about other things, too, because it kinda hurts how she never thinks she's good enough for anything. Especially since it's not true. She's good at so many things.

Maybe she'd be the *best* at something if she would just pick one thing, but that's not Nicole. She likes to bounce around and do everything. Another thing we're opposite about. I like to focus on something until I'm really good at it.

I know it doesn't make any sense, but I can't help feeling kinda guilty for being away so long. And for getting into the summer program at Ainsley in the first place. I worked hard and got to go away and have this amazing experience. Nicole works hard on so many things and never has a lot to show for it.

And now I'm supposed to tell her about the offer from Ainsley, the one that could take me away for all of eighth grade? For all of high school?

"What's wrong?" Nicole asks. "You thinking about your grandma?"

I kinda nod, and instantly feel bad for lying. Why *wasn't* I thinking about Grandma? She used to love me.

But there's no reason to ruin our first sleepover in seven weeks. I don't wanna be sad. I wanna have a good time with my best friend. Anyway, I can't do anything about Grandma right now. And I don't have to make a decision about Ainsley. Not today.

So why even say anything?

No, I don't like keeping secrets. I don't. But the thing is, secrets aren't a new thing. Not for me.

I was real little, living in Baltimore with Mom and Grandma and Mom's brother, Raymond. Dad was still in the Marines and he was always away somewhere, so most of the time, it was just the four of us in the house.

I liked Uncle Raymond. He was a teenager, but he let me play with him. He never treated me like a baby.

It was me and him, always together. Me and him always trying to do what we wanted, playing games and avoiding trouble with Grandma.

Me and him always keeping secrets.

We were silly and sneaky, creeping around the house, trying not to get caught. I was his little sidekick.

Sometimes Grandma would chase him away from me, tell him he was too old to be playing with a little kid, but there wasn't anyone else in the house for me to play with. If Uncle Raymond didn't play with me, I would have been alone.

And with Dad gone and Mom working all the time, being alone would have been the worst thing.

By the time my face is scrubbed clean and I'm dressed for bed, Nicole is talking me to death about everything that happened while I was gone. Like *everything*!

"Ayla has these party things on Saturday nights," she says, putting on some pajama shorts. "Not really *parties*, but her mom fixed up their backyard, so everyone goes over there and hangs out and listens to music."

All I say is, "Oh."

Nicole looks at her phone, then types something. "Gina is so stupid," she says, laughing. "She's spending the night with Ayla, and they're gonna stay up all night learning how to read tarot cards."

I put my satin bonnet on, grab *Breath, Eyes, Memory*, and crawl into the pullout bed.

For about fifteen, twenty minutes I let her spend time on her phone while I read, just so she can deal with everyone else. Then I close the book and say, "Okay, I'm ready. Tell me about Anthony."

"Really?" She flips over on her side, facing me.

I laugh a little and try to show that I'm really happy for her. "Yeah!"

"He's so sweet," she says. "You'll see when you meet him tomorrow. He's different than the boys around here. He stands out, you know."

"Yeah." I nod. "Does he like doing anything else besides baseball?"

"Well, he likes being with me." Nicole does that thing where she poses like she's some kinda fancy model or something.

That always makes me laugh.

Then she tells me all about Anthony, how he and his mom have been having trouble so she sent him to live with his uncle. And that Anthony has changed a lot since he's been here. He's focusing on baseball now, and he likes taking care of his uncle's dogs. "And he's such a good dancer. I tried to get him to dance with us at the festival, but he didn't wanna be the only boy."

"He would have gotten a lot of attention," I say.

"That's what *I* said!"

I like seeing her this happy. It seems like she and Anthony have a lot of fun together. Sometimes, when I'm with a boy, it's like I think too much. Like after the party last night. Why couldn't I just—

"Everything okay?" Nicole asks.

"Huh?"

"You're acting kinda, I don't know, different. Not different, just quiet."

"I had a long day, that's all." Not a lie. I *am* tired. "We had a party last night, and then I had to wake up early to pack the rest of my stuff."

"Tell me about the party! What was it like?" Suddenly, Nicole seems interested in Ainsley.

So I tell her everything about the party. The food, the music, and the boys. That's what she's really interested in. I tell her about Isaiah, the boy from Kentworth and how we danced practically the whole night together. I tell her how much fun it was, how good it all felt.

And that's when I stop. When the party was over. When I should have just gone back to my room.

I wish I could tell her. But I don't want her thinking I'm slipping back to my old ways. She thinks I've gotten better. I thought so, too.

I'm not sure what time I fall asleep, but in the dark, late at night, I wake up and see Nicole lying on her back, texting. "Go to sleep," I tell her. "You're gonna see him tomorrow."

"One minute," she says. Then she giggles at whatever's on the screen and types something else. "Anthony can't sleep."

I flip over, away from her, so she won't think I'm trying to read their romantic conversation.

A few minutes go by and all I hear is more giggling.

I know Nicole doesn't think I understand anything about boys. I never had a boyfriend, and I don't spend all day thinking about getting one. That's true. But that doesn't mean I don't like them. I do.

But it's complicated.

Back in fifth and sixth grade, I used to be like all the other girls. It was fun passing notes about who liked who, and which boy was the cutest. All of that. But when I started thinking about everything, I knew it wasn't that easy and fun. It starts that way, but it doesn't end like that.

"I'm done," Nicole says, and the light from her phone goes off. She settles back under her covers. "He's nervous about the game tomorrow, even though he won't admit it. I told him we'll come and bring him some good luck."

I turn around to face her. "What's it like having a boyfriend?" I whisper.

It's hard to see her in the darkness. The only light is a little strip coming in from the side of the window that the blinds don't cover all the way.

"You'll find out soon enough," she whispers back. "Anthony told me he has a friend for you."

I sit up. "What? Did you—?"

"No! I just told him you were back, and—"

"And I need help getting a boyfriend?"

"No, I didn't say that." She sits up, too, and she reaches over and rubs my arm a little. "I just said my best friend was back from boarding school camp or whatever, and did he know any boys that she could—"

"Oh my God!" I don't know what to feel. "You're making me seem like I'm desperate, like I can't get a boyfriend on my own or something."

"Does that mean you and Jarrett are finally gonna—"

"Would you stop with that already? Me and Jarrett are friends. That's it." I hop outta bed. I need to get outta that room, even for a few minutes. "I'm going to the bathroom," I say.

"Don't be mad," Nicole says, but her voice has a little bit of a laugh in it. "I'm just trying to—"

"Forget it," I say quickly. "It's okay. But can we just—"

"I'm done. No more boyfriend talk."

"Good." I leave the room and head down the hall. Mrs. Valentine's bedroom door is cracked and the light is still on, and the sound on the TV is low. I tiptoe past and go to the bathroom.

It's not until I'm inside that I feel I can breathe. I used to be able to do this. I used to be able to keep it together. But more and more, I can't.

I'm losing it.

· · · · ·

The best thing about sleepovers at Nicole's house is breakfast. The worst thing is Mrs. Valentine serves breakfast at 6:30.

Doesn't matter though. It's worth getting up for.

This morning she makes French toast stuffed with cream cheese and caramelized bananas. My eyes roll back in my head with the first bite. "You're killing me, Mrs. Valentine," I tell her. "Like, this is to die for!"

"I'm testing it out for the bakery."

Nicole gives her a thumbs-up. "Definitely go for it."

I just nod. I don't wanna stop eating long enough to say anything else.

After breakfast, me and Nicole are so full we both crawl back into bed with smiles on our faces. "I'm so happy I'm back," I tell her, my eyes closing.

"Me too," she says. "Mom makes better breakfasts when you're around."

A few hours later, after we're dressed, Mrs. Valentine takes us over to Broad Street, where all of Nicole's favorite stores are. And she doesn't stay with us. Even though she doesn't work on Sundays, she stops by her bakery to check on everything so we can shop alone. My mom slipped forty dollars in my pocket last night, so I'm actually able to buy something, but I'm not sure I wanna spend it on clothes for school. Especially since I'm not sure what school I'm going to.

But Nicole doesn't know that yet.

"There's so much cute stuff in here!" Nicole says, way too excited for the $9.99 store. They have their fall clothes out already, but

Nicole goes straight for the leftover summer stuff, which is on sale for $7.99. She picks up a yellow shirt with fringe on the short sleeves. The writing on the front says, *I Make My Own Sunshine*. "This is so me." She holds it up to her.

I nod. "I like it. Is that for school?"

"No, for today. Something Anthony hasn't seen me in yet." She looks at herself in the mirror and poses.

"He's gonna be busy playing baseball, not looking at your clothes."

"You don't know him," she says, grinning at herself in the mirror. "He notices everything I do."

"Get it. It looks nice."

"I am." She looks around. "What about you? See anything you can wear at school? You definitely need some eighth-grade clothes."

Like there's a big difference between seventh-grade clothes and eighth-grade clothes.

I walk around the store looking through all the racks. Nicole's right about there being a lot of cute things here, but where am I even shopping for? Am I staying here or heading back to Ainsley?

I pick up a random aqua shirt. It doesn't have any writing on it, but it has three little butterflies on one shoulder. Definitely not something I would wear to school, but maybe on the weekends.

I look over at Nicole. She shakes her head, so I put it back. Whatever. I already have enough clothes.

Nicole buys the yellow top and goes into the dressing room to put it on so she can wear it to the baseball game. And it looks great on her. Of course.

Shopping with Nicole takes forever. We go from one store to the next, then end up at the drugstore. She drags me to the makeup aisle and practically makes me buy a lip gloss that she says will make my lips *pop*. The only reason I buy it is because I actually like the color.

As we're leaving the last store, we see a group of boys walking right toward us. Nicole straightens up and eyes them. "Did they get cuter?" she whispers, kinda like a ventriloquist.

"Um, I don't think so," I say, trying not to move my lips either.

They're the same boys we went to school with forever. Only they're a grade ahead, so I guess they're technically high school boys now. But still.

As we get closer, one of the guys, Aaron, says, "Nicole and Caprice. Like peanut butter and jelly."

Nicole bats her eyes and kinda purrs, "Which one am I?"

Another boy looks at her butt and says, "Definitely jelly!" And they all laugh.

Nicole covers her mouth like she's embarrassed, but still, she can't hide that wide smile. She grabs my arm and we run down the street, and it's only until we're far enough away from the boys that we stop and she lets herself laugh. "I can't believe that just happened," she says. "That was crazy!"

But she loves it.

It takes a while for her to calm down. Then she says, "Those boys are so stupid. I thought high school boys would be more mature, but . . ." She shakes her head. "Good thing I have Anthony."

She *has* him?

Nicole looks at her watch, then puts her arm around me. "C'mon," she says. "Let's go find my mom. We have to get to the baseball field by one. No, twelve forty-five. I wanna be there when Anthony and the team run out on the field. I love that part!"

That's when I remember. I'm going to a baseball game.

•—•—•—•—•

I know which one is Anthony even before Nicole squeals. As the boys run onto the field, Nicole's new love is easy to spot. He's the coolest boy I've ever seen. Tan skin, dark hair, sideburns, handsome face. And way more confident than the other boys on the team.

As the other kids take the field and start warming up, Anthony takes his time walking onto the pitching mound. The kid has swagger!

Next to me, Nicole giggles. Then when Anthony turns around to face the bleachers, she waves like she's out of her mind. When he doesn't seem to notice her, she jumps up, still waving. "Over here!" she yells. That's when Anthony finally smiles. And what does he do next? He blows her a kiss.

And what does Nicole do?

She catches it. And places it on her heart. And sighs as loud as she can.

Then she sits down next to me and leans her head on my shoulder. "Isn't he the sweetest, most romantic, most—"

"Okay, okay," I say, laughing. "I get it. He's the best!"

"See? That's what I was trying to tell you."

I have to admit, Anthony does seem pretty great. Even as the team warms up, he keeps glancing over to Nicole and smiling. He's as into her as she's into him.

It's the first time this has happened. Usually Nicole is all into a boy who doesn't really pay her as much attention. But Anthony is different. This boy might be for real.

After the game is over and the Newark Newts celebrate their win, Nicole sits in the stands even as everyone else clears out of the bleachers. Anthony is still on the field, talking to some of the guys on the other team.

"Don't you wanna go over and say hi or something?" I ask her. "Or are we just gonna sit here all day?"

"My mom said I shouldn't always be the first one to talk to him or text him and stuff."

"You're listening to your mom now?"

"Only when it comes to boys. But she's right. I need to make them wait."

Them?

"Makes sense," I say, and take a look at my watch. "But I wanna meet him. And my dad will be here in twenty minutes."

Nicole stands up. "Alright, I made him wait long enough for me."

It turns out, Anthony isn't anything like all the other boys Nicole liked. I expect him to say hi to me and act like he doesn't know who I am even though Nicole probably told him all about me.

But not Anthony. He's the opposite. He's actually nice and friendly. When he sees me walking across the field with Nicole, he comes and meets us halfway, saying, "Caprice? Nicole talks about you all the time. Glad you're finally back, because she missed you."

Nicole play-slaps him on the arm. "Don't tell her that."

"Why not?" Anthony asks with a sly smile on his face. "She needs to know how you walked around all sad, waiting till she came back. And how many times did you say, 'I can't wait for you to meet Caprice!'?"

Nicole actually pouts. "I just wanted you to meet each other. That's all."

Anthony slips his arm around her waist. "I know." He pulls her close to him.

I guess they're cute together.

At the same time, I can't help feeling like I don't really need to be standing here watching this. They probably wanna hang out together, just the two of them.

"Hey, Rafa," Anthony calls out to the left fielder. "Come over here for a second."

Oh no. I forgot about this. The setup.

Rafa comes over to us, and right away, he's reaching his hand out for me. We shake. "Hey," he says. "Caprice, right? I like your name."

"Thanks," I say, forcing myself to smile. Rafa is kinda skinny, but he's cute. Nice smile. "Rafa—is that short for Rafael?"

"Yeah, but my dad's Rafael, so I got stuck being Rafa."

"I like it," I say. Next to me, I see Nicole and Anthony look at each other. Nicole's smile is like, *See? I knew they'd like each other.*

Because Nicole's watching, I talk to Rafa a little longer, about nothing really, just how long he's been playing baseball, how I once went to a Yankees game with my parents, how his team will be playing again next week, and will I be back?

I tell him I'm not sure yet, but that I had fun watching them today. Then his mom walks over to tell him they have to go, and I'm feeling kinda proud at how relaxed I was with him, how I seemed like a normal girl who knows how to talk to boys.

It was like that at the party with Isaiah, too. At first. Before I ruined everything.

I'm so good, Nicole is looking at me like she doesn't even know me. But she doesn't say anything. I'll probably hear how I did later, when it's just me and her.

I look at my watch. Knowing Dad, he's gonna be here in *exactly* seven minutes. On the dot. That's the Marine in him.

So I wait. I can't help wondering though. Does Nicole wish Dad would come and get me already? Does she wanna be here with Anthony alone?

Am I in their way?

When we get home, I grab my backpack and head up the stairs while Dad parks the car. Mom is sitting at the kitchen table doing some work on her laptop. It takes her a little while to even notice me there. "You have fun?" she asks, hardly lifting her head up from her spreadsheet and the rows and rows of numbers she's working on.

"Um, yeah."

"Good. Lana's coming by in a little while to tackle that nest on top of your head."

I head for the refrigerator.

"Wash your hands."

I sigh, but at the same time, I think I missed this. At Ainsley, it kinda felt like we were on our own. I mean, we had to be places at certain times and all that, but nobody was there telling us when to wash our hands, get ready for bed, or eat our vegetables.

It was definitely hard to get used to, but after awhile I adapted to it. It wasn't too hard because all I had to do was follow what everyone else did, especially the girls who go to Ainsley all year. They knew what to do.

I'm washing my hands when Dad comes in, carrying his heavy gym bag. The first thing he does is try to give Mom a kiss, but she moves away from him, laughing. "Ugh. Take a shower first!"

But that doesn't stop Dad. He goes in again for that kiss, and this time Mom lets him. "See?" Dad says. "I knew you couldn't resist me."

I dry my hands and lean against the counter and watch the two of them, and I don't wanna say or do anything. I want them to forget I'm here and be the way they probably were in Detroit.

Dad's still laughing when he heads down the hall. Makes me happy to see.

"Everything okay?" Mom asks me. I look over and it's like she's studying me. "You have fun with Nicole?"

"Yeah. It's just, I don't know, different. I think I've been away too long or something."

Mom and Dad must have gone shopping yesterday. The refrigerator is stocked.

"Did something happen?" she asks.

"No, not really." I grab a raspberry yogurt, get a spoon, and sit down next to her. "Busy?"

"Yeah. Doing payroll."

I wanna ask her how the business is doing, if things got better this summer. But I'm not sure the answer will be good, and I don't wanna stress her out.

"It feels good being back," she says. "Detroit was nice, but there's nothing like home, you know?"

I say yeah, but I don't really feel it the way she does. This house will never feel like home to me. But I can't tell her that either.

So I tell her about Mrs. Valentine's French toast and how crazy good it was.

"That woman can cook her butt off," Mom says. "Let's go to her bakery for breakfast tomorrow. See if Nicole is free."

"She probably has dance," I say, even though I'm not 100 percent sure what time anything is anymore. "The festival is next weekend."

"You and me then," Mom says.

I smile. "Yep."

Lana comes over about an hour later. Before I know it, she's sitting on the chair in the living room and I'm on the floor with a towel around my neck. She's given my hair a good wash and conditioning, and now she's separating my wet locs into sections with plastic clips so she can start retwisting the new growth. And there's been a lot in seven weeks.

"Girl, if you don't stop moving your head!" Lana puts her hands on either side of my head and straightens it out. "Why are you so restless?"

"I'm not restless," I say. It's just hard sitting still, bored. Especially since Mom is on the couch and she and Lana are talking, completely ignoring me. They're best friends like me and Nicole, and they have a lot to catch up on, too.

I think about Deja from Ainsley and text her.

> Sorry i didn't say goodbye

Five seconds later she texts back.

> where were you after the party you vanished

> i was with terra. how's kimberly? having fun in toronto?

> yeah. my little brother wants to marry her! he's 7!!!

> haha.

> will i ever see you again you coming back next summer

It takes me a minute to decide if I should do this, but I go ahead and tell her about Dr. Suzanne's offer. Half a second later I get a

> ☺ yay!!!

I laugh. It feels good that she's reacting that way, that she wants me back.

> my parents said yes already. but Dr S wants to hear from me this week.

and???

It takes me a few seconds to respond.

> i'll let you know what i decide.

you better come back we need you!!!

Between Terra and Deja, it's nice to know if I do go back, I'll already have friends.

Mom and Lana are laughing about something that I totally missed. Lana moves my head again and says, "This girl."

"She's probably tired," Mom says, like I'm not right there in the room. "She and Nicole were probably up all night talking and giggling."

"You know that's right!" Lana laughs. "So tell me, Caprice. What was it like up there at that fancy school?"

I take a deep breath. How do I answer that? Especially when something so perfect ended so bad.

"It was really great," I say. "Life-changing."

True.

"Your mom told me there was a big party on the last night."

"Yeah."

"Boys? Dancing?"

I nod . . . only to have Lana yank my head back in place again. *Ouch.*

Mom leans forward with an amused expression on her face. "Really? You danced with a boy?"

Why is she so surprised?

"Yeah. I mean, we were just having fun, like, acting silly. It was the last night, so . . ." I don't know what else to say.

"Was he cute?" Lana asks with a little laugh in her voice.

"I don't know. I guess so." He *was* cute. And funny. "He was one of the boys who went on the trip to MIT with us, so I already knew him. Kinda."

Mom tries to hide her smile. "Wow."

I'm sure she's gonna bring this up again. She's acting cool because Lana is here, but she's definitely gonna wanna know more. Not that she's against me dancing with boys or anything. It's the opposite. She probably thinks this means I'm growing up or something. Getting ready to start dating. All that.

Lana opens the loc gel, and the smell of shea butter and coconut hits my nose.

I missed this.

Mom's cell rings on the coffee table. "It's Aunt Gwen," she says. "That's weird."

Aunt Gwen is Grandma's sister.

Me and Lana are quiet while Mom talks. And even from just hearing one side, I can tell something is wrong.

Dad comes down the hall and steps into the living room. "What's going on?" he whispers to me.

"Aunt Gwen called," I say. "I think it's about Grandma."

Dad goes over and sits next to Mom, and he watches as she talks.

Grandma must be really sick.

By the time Mom gets off the phone, she has tears in her eyes.

"I can't believe this," she tells Dad. "Aunt Gwen says Ma's been sick for a while, but she didn't want a lot of people to know. Can you believe she has diabetes? And kidney problems. She's been on dialysis for years, and I didn't know any—" Mom shakes her head. "How could I not know anything about this? I mean, *dialysis?* That's serious."

Dad puts his arms around her. "Don't beat yourself up," he says. "How could you know?"

"That's the point. I *should* know. She's my mother."

"Don't do this, Nita. None of this is your fault."

Dad pulls Mom close, and even though she's sad, I'm glad Dad is home to help her. The thing is, he has to go back to Detroit, and Mom has to stay here with me. Of course, if I go back to Ainsley, Mom can go back to Detroit until the project they're working on is finished.

All I have to do is accept the offer, and they won't need to be separated again.

Grandma had glass dolls on a shelf in the living room. They were tiny, like three or four inches. Some of them were clear, see-through. But most of them were brown, and they wore colorful African dresses. A couple of them had scarves on their heads.

They were beautiful.

Over and over, I asked Grandma to lift me up so I could see them up close. I wanted to touch them. Play with them. But she would say they weren't that kind of doll. They were the kind you looked at but didn't touch. She said they could break too easily.

When I was little, I felt like one of those dolls.

I felt like I could break at any time.

• • • • •

Lana works in silence for a little while, which makes it easier to hear Mom and Dad, who are now talking in the kitchen. I hear the name Lovetta a lot, which means they're talking about Grandma. I'm trying to read, but it's too hard to focus.

"How are you liking that book?" Lana asks. I know what she's doing. She's trying to take my mind off what Mom and Dad are talking about.

"It's good," I say. "Kinda sad though."

"Yeah, I know. I read it a long time ago, and I still remember it. Finish it so we can talk about it later this week."

"Alright." I remember not to nod this time so I won't get my head yanked back again.

That's when I hear Dad say, "You're not listening." His voice isn't loud, but it's clear. "You're getting drawn back into your family's mess, Nita. You see that, right? And you know how I feel. I don't want Caprice going back to Baltimore."

My mouth flies open. *Me? What does this have to do with me?*

Lana stops twisting my hair, and we sit still and listen.

"I'm not getting drawn back in," Mom says. "But the woman is sick, and I'm her daughter. The hospital needs to talk to someone."

"It doesn't have to be you," Dad says. "Let your aunt deal with it. Let them get Raymond back in town."

"He's stationed overseas somewhere."

"Your mother made her decision, Nita. Remember when she threw you out of the house in the middle of winter with a four-year-old kid? Do you remember that? Because I do. And I'm not going to let you forget it."

Mom doesn't respond, and I can't hear anything else after that. I know Mom's feeling bad that she didn't know Grandma was sick, but it's not her fault. Grandma's the one who didn't want us anymore.

I was little, but I remember everything about that night. Mom didn't have anywhere to go, so we ended up at a motel in Baltimore. I remember jumping on the bed while Mom cried and talked to Dad on the phone, telling him everything that had happened that night. I didn't want everyone to be sad and mad. I wanted to have fun in that motel room. But inside I knew something really bad had happened. I knew we would never live in Grandma's house again.

I probably knew everything was about to change.

And I was right.

Dad's right, too. We shouldn't get caught up in Grandma's life, not after everything that happened.

And he's right that Mom should *definitely* not bring me back to Baltimore.

after baltimore

my world
closed in

my family
shrank

the three of us
stuck together
but
we lost everyone else.

⋯⋯⋯

After dinner, I sit next to Dad on the couch and we watch TV for a little while. Just some news show. When he lived at home, me and him used to watch *Jeopardy!* together every night, whenever he didn't have to work late or stay at work overnight.

Mom and Dad's argument from earlier is still hanging in the air. It's like everything changed. Dad didn't hold Mom's hand after that, and Mom hardly even talked at dinner.

I can't help but think this is all because of me. Not just the argument. *Everything.* Dad is mad at Mom's side of the family because of me. Dad's going back to Detroit by himself because of me. Mom's gonna be stuck here alone because of me, because I'm here.

If I go back to Ainsley, everything will be better.

"Your hair looks beautiful," Dad says, putting his hand under my chin and lifting my head so he can see my whole face. Lana has styled my locs into a high bun. "You look grown up." He puts his arm around my shoulder, and it's almost like he's reading my mind when he says, "I know you think this is a big decision, and it is, but it's a good thing, this offer. Not a lot of kids from around here get an opportunity like this, to go to a school like Ainsley. It's a gift."

"I know," I say. "I never thought something like this would happen to me."

"Why *not* you? You work hard and you're always looking out for others. You deserve good things. Dr. Suzanne told us about the speech you made."

"Yeah," I say. "It was supposed to be something about ways to help the less fortunate. Everyone was doing theirs on the need for different kinds of charities, but . . ." I shake my head. "I talked about growing up in Newark, and how sometimes people only see the problems here, not the good things. I told everyone that it's better to create leaders who are actually *from* areas like this because we're the ones who know what we need and what we don't."

"That sounds right." Dad is giving me that *proud dad* kinda look.

"I was so nervous, Dad. My leg was shaking the whole time!"

He laughs. "Dr. Suzanne said it was fantastic."

Being like this with him makes me wanna cry. "I don't want you to go," I whisper.

"I know. I wish everything was different, like before the business went—" He shakes his head. "You know, this has been a tough year for all of us."

I know.

My parents have their own business that provides security for large construction projects. They make sure nobody comes around to steal the building materials and the appliances and stuff. It's a twenty-four-hour-a-day job, and they have to hire a lot of security guards and off-duty cops, and use a lot of tech to make sure everything stays safe.

Last year, the business almost failed. My parents probably would have lost it if they didn't get hired by this company that builds apartment complexes all over the country. That saved us.

"Are you gonna keep working for this company?"

"Just got the next contract," Dad says. "Charlotte, North Carolina. I wish I could come back and work closer to home, but there's no work here right now. You know that, right?"

I nod.

"The way things are, I need to take what I can get."

I hate seeing Dad like this, sounding like he did something

wrong, or he let us down or something. It wasn't his fault what happened. It was just bad luck. "When are you coming back to visit us?" I ask him.

"I'm not sure," he says. "The Detroit construction project is at that crucial stage now. There's a lot of copper and expensive materials at the site, the kind of stuff thieves want to get their hands on. So I'm going to need to stay on top of things. I don't know if Doug and the guys can handle everything without me for too long."

Translation: He's not coming back.

"Why were you and Mom arguing? Was it about me?"

"Not you. *Baltimore.* Your mom's family." I can feel his body tense against mine. "I almost lost you once because of them, Caprice, and I don't want to risk that again."

I wanna tell him I'm not a baby anymore. I'm not gonna disappear in Baltimore again. But I don't say anything. I don't want this moment to end.

Me and Dad sit together until the news is over, until he says he needs to check in with his workers. Then he gets up and goes into the kitchen, back to his laptop.

I sit on the couch alone for a little while, trying not to get too upset. Things aren't getting worse. They're just going back to the way they were before I left for Ainsley. At least we had a little time together, me and Dad. That's something.

That's better than nothing.

holding on

sometimes i wish i could
talk
explain
tell
what happened
to me
a long time ago
so it's not inside
filling me up.

i want to stop
thinking about it
all the time

so I can be free
so I can be normal

After me and Mom have crepes for breakfast at Nicole's mom's bakery, Mom drops me off at the Center. Just like I thought, Nicole is in dance rehearsal. I watch them through the door again, just for a little while, but she doesn't notice me there. So I walk down the hall and check the schedule. There's so much stuff going on, but everything already started.

I can't just stand in the hall all morning. Then I see there's a new class. Well, new to me. Express Yo'self.

I shrug and make my way down to the room where it's meeting. It could be fun.

The first thing I notice when I open the door is there are only five kids in the class, three girls and two boys. They're all sitting at a round table with index cards in front of them. The second thing I notice is they're all older, like high school kids.

But nobody says anything when I walk in. One girl moves her mini backpack off a seat so I can sit next to her.

"Thanks," I say.

She smiles back. I know her. Kinda. She plays on the basketball team.

Everyone is looking at me, so I say, "Hi, I'm Caprice. Is it okay for me to stay?"

"Yeah," this boy on the other side of me says. "We're chill here."

The teacher looks young, like a college student. I think he was here last summer, too. "I'm Teddy," he says. "Like Oscar said, we're chill here. Just having fun. Sound good?"

I nod.

Teddy goes to the whiteboard. "This is my five-five-five writing exercise." He writes on the board: *Your day in five words, five letters each.*

"What's the other 'five'?" the other boy asks.

"The other five is, you got five minutes," Teddy says.

Everybody laughs.

A girl with light blue hair slides an index card and a pen to me. I mouth *thanks*. Then I just stare at the card for a few seconds.

The first word that comes to my mind is *crepe*. I can think of a bunch of other words, but none of them are five letters. Then I think about Mom and write *alone*. And I think of Ainsley and write *offer*.

A couple of minutes go by and I'm stuck. So that's what I write: *stuck*. I'm stuck in more ways than one. Stuck in this writing assignment. Stuck in the middle of two places I wanna be. Stuck in my own head most of the time.

But I'm here now, and I don't wanna think about anything else. So I write my last word: *happy*.

I'm not sure if I write it because I'm happy or if I just wanna remind myself to try to be happy. I wanna let go of everything going on and just have fun while I'm here. Because who knows how long I'm gonna stay.

After we finish writing our words, Teddy collects them and then gives each of us someone else's list. "Okay, now we're gonna write a short poem, fifty words or less, that incorporates all of these words."

Everyone groans.

"Oh yeah," Teddy says. "You got five minutes. And it has to make sense, y'all!" He laughs.

My list is really confusing:

SWEAT

TRASH

POWER

TIRED

WRITE

I'm trying to figure out how these words go together. But that's not the point. I just need to create something new, a poem that means something to me.

When we're done, Teddy makes us get up in front of the room to read our poems. Oscar reads my words, then his poem:

> Someone stuck a crepe in my refrigerator
>
> Which was weird cuz I was alone.
>
> But you offer me food, I'm happy.

Everyone claps, but I just laugh at how he made my words funny. When it's my turn, I'm not feeling too nervous reading my poem:

> When you're tired
>
> When you think your words are trash
>
> Don't sweat it
>
> When you write, you have power

It's not the best poem in the world, but for five minutes, it's okay. And everyone claps. One girl says, "Yes, there's power in writing."

After I read, I feel myself relaxing. I may be the only almost-eighth grader in the room, but I kinda feel like this is my group.

When the class is over, I go back to the rehearsal room to see if Nicole's finished. But she's not. I look through the window until finally she sees me and holds up five fingers. So I just sit on the floor, leaning against the wall, and read a few pages of my book.

When the door opens, Nicole runs out, her face covered in sweat. "Where were you this morning?"

"Eating your mother's food! My mom wanted to go."

"I get that!"

"She wanted me to invite you to come with us, and I wanted that, too, but—"

"But I was in dance," Nicole finishes for me.

"Yeah."

She shrugs. "I eat my mom's food every day. Don't worry about it." She takes the book outta my hand and looks at the cover. "Why are you reading so much? It's summer."

I'm not gonna tell her I'm reading it for Ainsley, so I just go, "It's really good."

"Whatever," she says.

A bunch of girls come outta the room, all of them sweaty and kinda messy. Next thing I know, me and Nicole are going with them down the hall to the bathroom. They wash their faces and put on deodorant, then they face the giant mirror and everybody fixes their hair and eyebrows and puts their earrings back in. Ayla has to be front and center. Her hair is in braids that go down her back, so all she has to fuss over is her face. She leans close to the mirror to apply her mascara. All the while she's talking about her weekend, and how she was forced to watch a boring documentary with her grandmother.

Gina laughs at everything she says. She's right next to Ayla, combing her hair. On the other side, Nicole is straightening the cuff on her shorts. All of this is getting worse as we get older. It used to be that we all went to the bathroom and fixed our hair a little bit before lunch. Now it's like they're getting ready for a fashion show.

All I can do is try on the lip gloss I bought yesterday. I have to admit, my lips actually do *pop*. I like it.

"Let me try it," Nicole says, and I pass it to her.

"Ooh, is that number 855?" Gina asks. "Can I try it?"

Nicole hands it over without even asking me. I watch Gina put it on and smile at herself in the mirror. "Cute!" She hands it back to me.

"So, Caprice, when did you get back anyway?" Ayla asks.

She's actually talking to me? "Um, Saturday."

"It sucks that you had to go away," she says, smoothing down her eyebrows. "I wouldn't wanna waste half my summer going to some school."

"I know, but it wasn't really *school* school."

"Oh, was it one of those schools where they teach you how to act like a lady?" She laughs at her own joke, which is strange because she asked me the same exact thing before I left for Ainsley. Ayla sticks her pinky out and pretends to sip tea. "You ready to meet the queen now?"

She said *that* before I left, too. Nothing changes around here.

"The pictures looked nice though," Gina says. "Like, fresh air and stuff."

I try not to react, but all I can think is, why did Nicole show them the pictures I sent her? I mean, they weren't really private or anything. I took most of them on the tour the first day of the summer program. I'm not sure why. Maybe I was just amazed by everything. Like, I couldn't believe it was all real.

Maybe I was just taking the pictures for myself at first. Then I texted Nicole a picture of the dorm building with the pretty garden on either side of the glass front doors. I wrote something about how beautiful Ainsley was, and she texted back that it looked like a college.

I sent her a bunch of pictures that day: the library, the little pond behind the gym, a stone bench outside the administration building. I wanted Nicole to be there with me. I didn't want her to feel like I'd forgotten about her.

Of course, I thought our texts and the pictures were just for her. I never thought she would show them to anyone else except maybe her mom.

"The most important thing." Ayla is talking to me again but still looking in the mirror. "What about the boys up there? What were *they* like? Rich?"

"There weren't any boys," I say. "It's an all-girls school."

That actually gets Ayla to stop looking at herself for once in her life. She turns around to face me. "All *girls*?" She's giving me a strange look. "Oh, that couldn't be me."

I wanna ask her why not. Is it so terrible to be around other girls? But what I say is, "It was fine. We got to see boys on trips and things."

Ayla breathes out a sigh of relief. "Good. 'Cause that would have been horrible."

Another minute of looking at themselves and then, "Okay, everybody ready." Ayla doesn't ask this. She *tells* them they're ready.

Then, again, I find myself trailing behind the girls outta the bathroom and down the hall, on our way to the cafeteria. We walk through the doors, past a group of boys standing together in a pack. None of the girls say anything to them or even look at them really. We head straight for the round table in the middle of the room.

This is different. We never sat here before I left. I guess the girls wanna make sure everyone is seeing them now.

Miss Lisa, who works in the cafeteria, starts telling everyone to line up, but me and Nicole hold the table while everybody else goes first. Nicole leans in close to me and says, "I never asked you—what did you think about Rafa? Super cute, right?"

"Yeah," I say. "And nice."

"If you want, we could all go out together, and you could get to know him better."

I shrug. "I don't know. Let me think about it."

Nicole smiles slyly. "Unless you're still thinking about Jarrett." She giggles.

I glance over to the table where Jarrett always sits, but he's not there yet, and for some reason I feel relieved. "Why did you show everybody the pictures I sent you?" I ask.

Nicole gives me a look. "Were they supposed to be secret?"

"No, I mean, that's not the point. I sent them to you. For *you*."

"Sorry." She says it like she's *definitely* not sorry.

"Where's Anthony today?"

"Working at his uncle's pizzeria." She actually pouts. "He can't come every day."

"He probably misses you."

"He better!"

That's when I see Jarrett come into the cafeteria with Ennis. They head straight for their table and Ennis pulls out the sketchbook he always has. Jarrett looks around, and the second our eyes meet, he freezes. I give him a little wave, and he smiles. But the rest of his body is still frozen. He didn't know I was back.

Even after I turn back to Nicole, I know Jarrett's eyes are still on me.

Finally, all the girls come back and Nicole stands up. "You coming?"

I pat my belly. "Your mom's food, remember?"

This girl, Yesenia, comes over to the table and drops her backpack on a chair. "I know I'm late, but you guys need to check out what we did outside on the basketball court. It looks like a giant Miró painting . . . if they had sidewalk chalk back in the olden days."

I have no idea who Miró is, but if I ask, that will just get Yesenia to go on and on about art and artists. I've made that mistake before.

Nicole tells her she can't wait to see it, and then the two of them get in line together. And I'm stuck there with the other girls. I probably should have gone with them even though I'm not hungry.

Because when Nicole's not around, the other girls don't even know I'm here.

watching

sometimes I watch jarrett
watch me
nicole says he loves me,
and she knows this for a fact.
she can tell by the way he looks at me,
the way he tries to talk to me,
how nervous he gets around me.
all of that is proof
of his love
if you ask nicole.

i wish jarrett didn't like me
or love me.
it makes me feel weird.
uncomfortable.

last year,
jarrett was just a boy
in my class.
now there's an invisible layer
on top of our friendship.

i know we're getting older
and things change,
but everything is changing really fast.

it would be nice if we could go back
to when jarrett looked at me the same way
he looks at everyone else.

‥ ‥ ‥

I can feel my phone vibrating in my backpack. It's after lunch and we've all changed into our gym clothes for volleyball. I'm wearing my white Ainsley Angel sweatpants, and I'm kinda glad nobody says anything about them.

We get to the gym early, so we're sitting on the bleachers watching Gina teach some girls how to do a back walkover. She's so flexible. No wonder she's so good at dance. I dig for my phone without letting anyone see. It's just a text from Mom.

> Got a call from Dr. Isidro. She asked for permission to contact you. Everything ok?

Dr. Isidro? It takes me a second to remember who that is. Then I remember she's the counselor at Ainsley. She came to our program on the first day and told us where her office was. She talked to us about how it's normal to feel homesick, especially for the kids who were far away from home for the first time.

Dr. Isidro said she was available to talk anytime if we needed it. She seemed nice.

I text Mom back.

> i'm ok. maybe it's abt coming back 2 AI.

> Dr. S probably wants her to find out if you're nervous about taking the offer.

> yeah prob

I don't put the phone back in my backpack, now that I know Dr. Isidro is gonna call. I slip it in my pocket and wait. Could this really be about the offer? Or is that just wishful thinking?

Does she know about Friday night?

Dr. Isidro calls not even ten minutes later. Vanessa, who teaches volleyball, just got here and we're forming groups, so nobody notices me grabbing my backpack and slipping outta the gym. I race down the hallway to the front doors before answering the phone.

"Hello?" I say.

"Caprice? It's Dr. Isidro, from Ainsley."

"Um, hi." I push open the door and step outside into the afternoon heat. It's gotten so much hotter. There are benches out there, but I'm too nervous to sit. I need to know what this is all about. "My mom said you wanted to speak to me."

"Yes," Dr. Isidro says. "I'm sorry I wasn't around on Friday night, but when I got back to work today, I found the note Terra left for me."

My mind is racing. I have no idea what she's talking about.

"I'm concerned about you," Dr. Isidro continues. "How are you doing now?"

"Uh, um. I'm alright." There are a few seconds of silence. It's like she's waiting for me to say more, but I don't know what.

"Okay, Caprice," she says. "Is everything going well now that you're back home?"

"Yeah, it's good. I'm at the community center in my neighborhood right now."

"And I hear you might be coming back to AI. How are you feeling about that prospect?"

"I'm still thinking about it. It's very exciting, a big decision."

Dr. Isidro laughs a little. "It's life-altering."

"I know! But it's hard because I'll be happy whichever decision I make."

Me and Dr. Isidro talk for another minute or two, about Ainsley and how I wasn't sure I was gonna like it at first, but how much I really loved it there.

Finally, she asks, "Is there anything going on that you'd like to talk about? You can talk to me, or I can help you find a counselor in Newark that can help you."

"I'm okay," I say again. "Really."

Dr. Isidro's voice gets even softer. "Okay, that's good to hear. But now that I called you, you have my number on your phone. Call me anytime."

"Okay," I say. "Thanks."

We say our goodbyes, and I click the phone off. Then I sit on the bench, replaying the phone call in my mind over and over. I have no idea what that call was about, or why Dr. Isidro treated me like someone who needs help or something. What does she know about me?

What did Terra's note say?

Without really thinking, I text Terra.

> dr i called me. what did you write in your note?

I sit out there, holding the phone, waiting for her to get my text and let me know what she did. A few minutes go by. I take my book out and try to read while I wait.

Not that long after, the girl with the light blue hair from Express Yo'self, who I now know is named Bree, walks outta the Center holding hands with Oscar. I guess they're boyfriend-girlfriend. As they get closer to me, Bree says, "That book is good, right?"

I nod. "So far, yeah."

Then Oscar says, "You coming back to class on Thursday? You're good."

Bree adds, "We're gonna work on some poems for the Cultural Festival, if you're into reading in public."

"I don't know about that," I say.

"Think about it," she says. Then they walk down the path to the sidewalk, never letting go of each other's hands.

It takes like ten, fifteen minutes. Then I see that Terra is texting me back.

call you later. ok?

She made me wait for that?

I slip the phone back in my pocket without responding. Why would she tell Dr. Isidro anything about me? And why didn't she tell me about that note?

● ● ● ● ●

After volleyball, me and Nicole leave the Center to go to the bodega. It's even hotter now, and the sun is beating down on my skin. We're trying to move as fast as we can, just to get to the air-conditioned store. "Why are we out here?" I kinda yell because it's *that* hot.

"For sunflower seeds!" Nicole says as we run into the store.

On the way back, we cut across the parking lot behind the stores, a shortcut that will get us back to the Center faster.

Right near the end of the lot, there are two men fixing a car, listening to loud rap music. We're not really close to them, but that doesn't stop one of them from calling out, "Girls! Girls! Y'all looking good!" The words slither outta his mouth, giving me the creeps. "What? Y'all ain't gonna stop and talk to me?"

We ignore him and keep walking even faster.

Then he yells, "You in the white pants, you ain't no angel. Not with a body like that!"

I inhale a lot of air and hold it inside.

That's when the other man says something really disgusting, and both of them start laughing.

Nicole grabs my hand and we run away, my heart beating fast the whole time. I'm still holding my breath, and now I feel sick inside.

"Just ignore them, Caprice," Nicole says, still holding my hand, pulling me down the street. "Don't let them bother you."

Finally, I gasp for air and take deep breaths.

Nicole's right. I can't let them get to me. I need to hold it together. I can't fall apart again.

I've told Nicole about this before, how it makes me feel when men look at me like that. I know most girls can just ignore it like Nicole does, but me, I can't. It gets inside my body, and it's hard to let it go.

Back at the Center, it takes me a while to stop thinking about why grown men would say something like that to girls, especially our age. All through drama class, my brain is stuck back there in the parking lot, and I can't stop seeing their faces and hearing their words.

Even in yoga class, when we're supposed to be clearing all our stress away and making our minds like water, I can't let it go. Good thing Nicole is there next to me, trying to make me laugh by deliberately wobbling during triangle pose and putting her hand on mine at the end of class as we lie side by side in reclining butterfly. She's trying to make me feel better. That's what she always does.

But no matter what, I'm never gonna get used to men doing that kinda thing. I shouldn't have to. It's not fair that girls even have to put up with stuff like that.

•••••••

After we left Grandma's house in Baltimore, we moved to Newark. The Marines still had Dad, so me and Mom stayed with Lana until he got back. We shared a small room, but I loved it because it was painted yellow, just like my room in Grandma's house.

I was almost five, but I was sad all the time. I missed Dad, and everything was different. I had to go to a new pre-K, and I didn't know anybody.

That's when I met Nicole. She knew everybody. Even back then she was the most popular kid at school. One day we were finger painting at our easels, and I didn't want to ask if I could go to the bathroom even though I had to go real bad. I didn't want everyone looking at me. I just wanted to be invisible.

So I tried to hold it as long as I could. I did. But I couldn't. And I actually stood there and peed on myself. Then I covered my face with my hand and tried not to think about what I did.

I was in pre-K. I wasn't a baby. I knew how to go to the bathroom. Something like that wasn't supposed to happen to a big girl like me.

But it did.

And my teacher, Mrs. Mastromatteo, had to stop what she was doing, tell the rest of the class to keep painting, and take me into the bathroom to help me take off my tights and clean up. She let me keep my dress on because it wasn't wet, but she had to wash out my tights. Then, later, she hung them on the same clothesline where all of our finger paintings were drying.

It was so humiliating. I didn't want anybody to look at me, even when the teacher tried to make me feel less ashamed by saying that maybe I was coming down with a fever, and sometimes things like that happen when you're getting sick, that it was nothing to be embarrassed about.

Later during playtime, I knew nobody would want to play with me. But I was wrong. Nicole didn't care. She came over to me with two baby dolls, gave me one, and took my hand and led me over to the playhouse area. The next thing I knew I had almost forgotten about my tights hanging there for everybody to see. I knew I had a friend.

Walking out of yoga class, me and Nicole are right behind Jarrett and Ennis. She nudges me, like she wants me to say something to Jarrett, but I just glare at her. I don't need her to push me to talk to someone who's been my friend since we were little kids.

In the hallway, I glance over at Jarrett, and he's already looking at me, so I turn away really fast, and for some reason, my heart starts racing.

This makes no sense.

So I just turn to him and say, "Hi." That's it. Something simple to get us back to talking like we used to.

Jarrett's eyes get wide for a second, like he's surprised I said anything. Then he goes, "Oh, yeah. Hey. You're back."

I can't help but giggle. He's so weird.

"What?" Jarrett asks. "What's so funny?"

"You!" I'm still laughing.

Now he laughs, too. "Why does everybody say I'm funny when I'm not even trying to be?"

"Maybe you should be a comedian."

"Nah," he says. "Not me. Don't forget. I'm gonna be a famous movie director."

"Come on, Jarrett," Ennis says, leaning closer to him. "We don't wanna be late for *you-know-what*."

I don't ask what they're gonna be late for because there's only one thing the boys get all secretive about. Man Group.

"I gotta go," Jarrett says to me. "Um, I'll see you, you know, around." And they're gone, racing around the corner to their stupid group.

I head straight upstairs to Mrs. Prajapati's office. She runs the whole center, so she's always busy, but I'm willing to wait.

Her door has a big silver name plate:

NAREEN PRAJAPATI
DIRECTOR

The door's usually open, but not today. I knock real light, just in case she's too busy to deal with kids today.

But I hear, "Come in."

I step inside, and right away Mrs. Prajapati smiles and jumps up. "Caprice!" She comes around from behind her desk, and the next thing I know, she's giving me a hug. "You're back," she says. "Tell me all about your experience. Was it everything you imagined?"

I take a deep breath and smile, too. "So much better than that." I fill Mrs. Prajapati in on all the highlights of my time at Ainsley, telling her about the leadership program, our college trip, and the speech I made about growing up in Newark.

"I met so many girls from around the world," I tell her. "My roommate Terra is from New Zealand!"

"Is?" Mrs. Prajapati asks me, one eyebrow raised.

"I mean *was*."

"Are you thinking about going back?"

How did she do that?

"I, um . . ." I don't even know where to begin. But she's waiting to hear what I'm gonna say. "The head of the school offered me a scholarship, but—"

Mrs. Prajapati gasps. "Oh my goodness. That's—"

"I'm not sure if—I don't know if I wanna go yet. I mean—"

"Why not?" She's looking at me like I've lost every bit of my mind.

"Because . . . I don't know."

Mrs. Prajapati is still staring, so I feel like I need a better answer. I say, "I don't know if I wanna leave school and my teachers and everybody here at the Center. I never heard of Ainsley until one of my teachers told me about the summer program. And I probably wouldn't have gotten accepted if you and my principal didn't write letters of recommendation. I don't wanna leave everybody who's been looking out for me since I moved to Newark. Everybody here pushes me to do better, so why should I leave?"

"The reason we push you is because we know what you're capable of."

"I know."

"There's nothing wrong with going to new places and trying new things, Caprice."

"But the whole point was to go there and learn to be a leader back in our own communities, not to *stay* there. They don't need more leaders in places like Ainsley. Trust me."

"I know this decision is difficult," Mrs. Prajapati says. "But if you go, it won't mean you've turned your back on us."

"But what if—" I shake my head because I know she's gonna say I shouldn't think this way, that I'm being silly. "What happens if I get there and I wanna come home?"

Mrs. Prajapati smiles. "You can always come home. Your mother, your friends, and all of us here at the Center will be right here if you do."

That gets me to smile, too. "Okay," I say. "Makes sense."

Mrs. Prajapati walks back around to the other side of her desk. "You've been in this office for three minutes and you haven't asked me about the new group you proposed yet."

I'd almost forgotten. And that's why I'm here. "So?"

Mrs. Prajapati grins. "Your Woman Group has been approved. We were waiting for you to get back."

I actually clap my hands. "Yay!"

"The group starts on Friday and we have a wonderful leader already lined up. All we need to do is make sure there are enough girls interested." She puts a sheet of paper on a clipboard and writes WOMAN GROUP on top. "I'd like you to get fifteen signatures on this." She hands me the clipboard.

"Fifteen?"

"I need those signatures tomorrow. I can't go ahead with the group if there's no interest."

"No problem," I say, trying extra hard to sound confident. "I'll get those signatures. It's not fair that the boys have Man Group and we don't have a group just for us."

"You'd better get started."

I thank Mrs. Prajapati and practically run outta the room. I can't waste time. I really need a Woman Group. I just hope the other girls feel the same way.

Before I head home, I go to the computer room to make some flyers. I need to get the word out if I'm gonna get fifteen signatures in one day.

I'm only there for about five minutes, scrolling through fonts, when the door opens.

"Sorry," I hear. "I didn't know anybody was in here."

It's Jarrett.

"No, it's okay." I turn his way. He looks like he's ready to leave. "Come in. I'm not doing anything private or anything."

"I can come back."

"Jarrett, the computers are for everyone. And all I'm doing is looking for fonts and pictures for my flyer."

It's hard to explain why, but I'm glad he's here.

Jarrett comes in and sits down at a computer three seats away from me. I giggle, but I don't say anything. He's right. If anyone comes in and sees us sitting next to each other, next thing we know, everyone's gonna think we're a couple or something.

"What kinda flyer are you . . . I mean, if it's not personal or—"

"Stop doing that," I say. "Do you have something important to do? Because I won't disturb you."

"I just wanna work on our movie."

"You did it? You made the cartoon?"

"Almost finished. Ennis did all the artwork, but we wrote it together. It's really funny."

"I can't wait to see it," I tell him.

"I need to find some sound effects and music I can use." He logs onto his computer and opens the music app.

On my computer, I type *WOMAN GROUP* big in the center of the page, then change the font a few times to find the right one. "How was your summer?" I ask Jarrett when the weird sounds he's playing die down for a few seconds.

"Summer's not over. We still have a week and two days."

I laugh. "I know what you mean. It went by fast. I missed everything."

"But you had fun at that school, right?"

I nod. "Yeah, it was good."

All of a sudden loud music plays from his computer. It sounds kinda creepy *and* funny at the same time.

"I like that," I say.

"Yeah. It's exactly what I need for the last scene."

I keep typing:

A Group Just for Girls

Starts This Friday!

See Caprice to sign up!!!

The font looks nice, but the flyer is boring. I sit back and think of ways to make it pop.

"You want help?" Jarrett asks.

I ask him if he knows how to find good artwork. "I need a fancy border or something. So when I post this around the Center, girls will notice it."

"Ennis could create something."

"Yeah!" Ennis has done a bunch of posters and banners and stuff. "He's so talented. Think he'll help?"

"I'll go get him."

Jarrett stands up, and me and him look at each other for a few seconds, just smiling. I don't know what he's thinking. But I'm thinking, I missed him.

• • • • •

After Jarrett and Ennis help me create the flyer, I print out a bunch of copies and hang them up around the Center. Then I text Mom that I'm on the way home. I walk the long way again, past the stores. I'm about two blocks away from home when my phone vibrates. It's Terra calling me back.

The first thing she says is, "I couldn't talk before because I was with my mum."

"I figured." My voice comes out flatter than I want it to. I'm not angry with her. At least I don't know if I am yet, because I don't know why she went to Dr. Isidro without telling me. "I didn't mean to interrupt your vacation. I just wanna know why you left that note. What happened?"

"What happened is I panicked," she says, and now I can hear the echo that lets me know she's in the bathroom. "You were so . . . I couldn't get you to calm down. I knew you didn't want anyone to know, so—"

"So you *told* the school counselor?" I can't believe what I'm hearing.

"You were having an emotional breakdown or something, Caprice. I thought Dr. Isidro could help. She said if we talked to her, she'd keep everything we told her private, remember?"

"And she wasn't there, so you left her a note?"

"She was at the party. I thought she might come back to her office and get the note. I didn't know she wouldn't see it until today."

I'm silent. Just hearing her talk about Friday night brings back all those emotions I still can't understand.

"Are you still there?" Terra asks, and she sniffs loudly. She's crying. "I thought I was, I don't know. I wanted to get you help. I didn't know what to do, how to help you. Don't be mad."

I breathe out hard. How can I blame her for trying to help me? "I'm not mad," I tell her. "I know I scared you. You were only trying to help."

She sighs. "That's all I wanted."

"I know. Thanks. Seriously, thanks."

Everything that happened was my fault. Not hers. After holding everything together for so long, I let go. I broke.

Can't let that happen again.

Terra and I talk for a few more minutes as I walk the rest of the way home. She fills me in on her trip, and I tell her about breakfast.

"We have a cooking elective at Ainsley," she says. "It's just for fun. Maybe we can try to make those crepes."

"That would be fun."

"Have you made your decision yet? You coming back?"

"I'm not sure," I say. "I'm still thinking."

"Well, think fast!"

Hearing her voice makes me think about all our conversations in the darkness of our dorm room. And it makes me remember how much I loved being there.

•–•–•–•

Since it's just me and Mom now, we make chicken fajitas together and eat in the living room while watching a movie on Netflix. With Dad gone, it's just like it was before I went away, except tonight we're both kinda not there. Part of me is still thinking about what Terra said, how much I freaked her out the other day. The more I try not to think about it, the more I can't stop myself.

What happened to me that night?

Mom gets a couple of texts from her family in Baltimore, and the hospital calls during the movie, just to get permission to do some kinda medical test on Grandma.

"Did you talk to the counselor?" Mom asks me after the movie is over and we're cleaning up the kitchen. "What's her name? Dr. Isidro?"

"Yeah. She just wanted to see if I was nervous or anything about coming to Ainsley. You know, checking up on me." Then I add, "She's nice."

"Oh, okay."

I can tell she's distracted by the way she's cleaning the counter, wiping the same area over and over. "Is Grandma okay? Is she gonna be alright?"

Mom half shakes her head, half shrugs. "I don't know. It's serious."

I look down, not knowing what to say or do. I wish none of this was happening.

Mom asks, "Do you remember your grandmother?"

I nod. "Yeah, a little."

That's a lie. I have a lot of memories from back then, and Grandma is in most of them.

"I know your father doesn't want you going back there. I don't want that either, believe me. So let's pray that Grandma gets better."

I nod. "Okay."

By this time next week, I could be back at Ainsley, all settled into my dorm room. Safe. I will pray Grandma won't need Mom in Baltimore before then.

It didn't just happen that one time in pre-K. It happened before we moved to Newark, too. In Grandma's room, back when we still lived with her.

I didn't want to sleep in Grandma's room anyway. I wanted to sleep in my own room, the one that used to be Mom's room, the one with the pretty yellow walls and all my stuffed animals on the bed. But Grandma told me I had to sleep with her. In her room. She said she wanted to make sure I was safe.

Grandma slept with this plastic thing over her nose and mouth and a machine on the side of the bed that was supposed to help her breathe or something. It was scary. It made her look funny, like an elephant. I thought she would stop breathing and I wouldn't know what to do.

One night, I woke up and had to go to the bathroom. I got outta bed and tried to open the door. I turned the doorknob and pulled, but I couldn't get the door to open. I tried over and over, but the door wouldn't budge.

I tried to wake Grandma up. I shook her and shook her, but she was sleeping too hard. And when I called, "Grandma, Grandma," she couldn't hear me. Nothing worked. I couldn't wake her up, and I couldn't get out. So I stood there by her bed, not knowing what to do.

And it happened. I peed all over myself and all over the rug and I couldn't do anything except get back in the bed, soaking wet, and try to sleep. But I couldn't. I stayed awake the rest of the night, dreading the moment Grandma would see what I had done. Even as a little kid, I knew it wasn't my fault, but that didn't stop me from feeling ashamed. I worried that she was going to yell at me or think I was a baby.

But that didn't happen. And she didn't change her mind and tell me I had to go back and sleep in my own room. Even after what I had done, she never let me sleep in my own bed again.

I get to the Center early so I can try to get most of the girls to sign up for Woman Group as soon as they get there. It's busy already. Everybody is doing something different, running up and down the halls. The band is practicing their songs in the music room, and some of the preschoolers are outside in the back of the Center playing games. The senior citizens are there, too, having breakfast in the cafeteria and using the computers.

I pick the best spot, right under the schedule, where I can see everybody coming and going, and I stand there with my clipboard waiting for middle school girls.

Down the hall, three boys are running, trying to jump up and touch the EXIT sign over and over for no reason. Then, from the other end of the hall, little kids follow one of the group leaders around the corner from the preschool to the gym. And there's some loud drumming coming from a classroom somewhere.

"Alicia! Alicia!" I call out to a girl down the hall. She's carrying a large plastic bin full of colorful yarn. But all she does is wave at me and keep walking.

A few minutes later, a girl who's going into seventh grade walks in my direction. "Janelle, can I ask you something?" I hand her my flyer.

She looks at it and reads, "'A group just for girls.' Um, put me down for a no." She hands the flyer back to me and walks away.

Talk about rude.

I wish I could say those are the only girls who are like that, but most girls I try to talk to about Woman Group are either too busy to talk or not interested at all.

Finally, a girl named Savannah comes up to me. "What's this about?"

"You know how the boys have their secret Man Group? Well, this is for us. It's a place for us to talk about girl stuff."

She looks at the flyer for a little longer and says, "What do we have to talk about?"

The way she looks at me, like she really can't think of anything girls need to talk about, I don't know why, but it kinda gets to me. "Girls have a lot going on," I say, and for some reason, my voice cracks. "We have to deal with a lot of things sometimes."

I look down and try to keep it together.

"I'll think about it," she says. "But I'm late for crocheting." She runs down the hall, and I think I need to stop standing here. I need a break.

I look up at the board to see what I can do.

"You okay?" Nicole comes up behind me in the hall, slipping her arm around my shoulder. I didn't even notice that dance had taken a break and everybody is in the hall. I'm just staring up at the activity schedule on the wall, still holding my clipboard.

"Yeah, I'm okay," I say, probably a little too quickly. I blink away my tears and try not to face her until I can hide my feelings a little better.

"Get any signatures yet?"

"It's just . . . I don't know why this is so *hard*." I drag the last word out like it's a joke.

"You know how girls are around here. Everybody wants to do what everybody else is doing. They don't wanna be first." She slides the clipboard out of my hand and signs her name big on the first line. Nicole Valentine. She even puts hearts instead of dots over her *i*'s. "There. Now everybody can follow me!" She smiles, so confident.

This is why she's my best friend.

There's a thud as one of the boys down the hall falls and lands on his butt. And of course his friends laugh at him because that's what they do.

I shake my head. Just when I think I missed having boys around all the time, they remind me why an all-girls school can't be a bad thing.

Nicole laughs at the boy, too. "Nothing changed while you were gone. As you can see, the stupid boys are still stupid."

I'm quiet.

"Seriously," she says. "Are you okay? Because I don't— You know. I don't want you going back to the way you were last year."

I look down. "I'm not."

I can't.

Seventh grade was hard. I drifted away from everything and everyone. Dad was gone. Mom was sad all the time. And me, I was sinking. I couldn't stop myself from thinking and feeling, and all of it kinda choked me.

That was when I got even more into school. Studying took my mind off the hard stuff. It gave me something else to think about besides me. Nicole knew something was wrong with me, but I couldn't talk about it. I just needed to keep it inside and wait.

So now, seeing Nicole look at me with those same sad, worried eyes, I quickly tell her, "I'm fine. For real."

It takes her a second to give me a relieved smile. "Good. Okay, well, I have to get back to dance," she says. "Wanna come? It's not too late to learn the dance in time for the festival."

"No, I need to get these signatures."

"Okay, but have *fun*." She squeezes my arm. "Be happy!" Then she takes off down the hall.

I'm only there a few more minutes when Miriam comes into the Center with her mom. They hug at the door, and Miriam heads down the hall in my direction. "Caprice!" she calls out, so happy to see me. "I made something for you!" She reaches into her backpack and takes out a plastic bag. Inside is a pretty necklace with light blue and pale pink beads. "This is for you, for being my buddy."

I bend down so she can slip it over my head. "Perfect," I say. It's really cute. "You made this yourself?"

"Yep. In jewelry class."

"I love it. Thanks!" I give her a hug. "You're really talented."

"Anyone can make one," she says. "Hey, come to art with me. We're making stuffed animals."

The thing I like about Miriam is, she doesn't wait for me to answer. She takes my hand and pulls me down the hall with her, which is probably a good thing since I need to clear my mind. And I have nothing else to do.

• • • • • •

I remember last year, in the middle of all my sadness, something happened at the elementary school across from our school. We were in homeroom, and as soon as the principal got on the microphone, we knew it was something serious, not the regular, everyday announcement. She almost sounded scared.

Dr. Johnson told us that a man approached a third-grade girl from the elementary school and tried to lure her into a gray van. The girl was walking to school by herself, but she screamed at the man and ran away. The principal told us that if anybody approached us, we should avoid him and, if we had a phone, call 911. She said a man like that needed to be in jail.

After the announcement, everybody started talking, but I kinda zoned out. I started having a hard time breathing. Thinking.

I made it through homeroom and even a few minutes into math, but my head was foggy and I had to fight to keep myself from getting dizzy. But it was my stomach that was taking all my attention. Everything I had eaten for breakfast felt like it was churning, and it hurt. I sat there, listening to Mrs. Lipsinki talk about irrational numbers, but I was doubling over. I felt a metallic taste in the back of my throat, and I knew I didn't have any time left. I had to get out of there and to the bathroom immediately.

So I jumped up and ran out of the room without saying anything. I ran down the hall to the bathroom as fast as I could. I made it to the bathroom but not the toilet. I threw up in the garbage can and on the floor. Mrs. Lipsinki came into the bathroom after me a few seconds later. "Caprice, are you okay? Do you need the nurse?" She stopped and looked at the mess I'd made on the floor.

I was leaning against the wall, trying to catch my breath and hoping the waves of nausea would stop and I wouldn't throw up again. "I don't know what . . . I messed up my shirt."

Mrs. Lipsinki wet a paper towel and squeezed out the excess water. "Here." She handed it to me, and I wiped my face and then my shirt. I felt awful. There was no way I could go back to class.

So I didn't. I went to Dr. Johnson's office, and she called Mom, who picked me up about a half hour later. She made me some broth, gave me some saltine crackers we had in the back of the cabinet, and made me drink Alka-Seltzer.

That night as I lay on the couch under a blanket, the story of what happened at the elementary school came on the news. I sat there frozen, tears streaming down my face. I felt scared, unsafe in my own home. I knew I wasn't a little kid. A man in a van wouldn't be able to trick me into going inside. But still, it felt like there were so many of them out there, so many men wanting little girls. And even though I wasn't a little girl anymore, I had been a little girl. And just like the little girl at school that day, I wasn't safe then either.

After that, I couldn't help getting kinda obsessed with gray vans and scary men. I looked for the van everywhere and stayed away from every man I didn't know.

And I watched the news all the time, waiting to see if other girls were approached by men like that, or if any little girl had gotten snatched. I wanted to see the owner of that gray van in handcuffs so I could feel better, but that never happened.

It got bad. It got to the point that it was hard for me to think about anything else. Some nights, I would just lie in bed, not sleeping, just thinking.

After a couple of weeks, I did what I had to do, just so I could get through the day and night without worrying all the time. I organized.

I talked to the other seventh graders (and some eighth graders, too) *and signed up a bunch of volunteers to be buddies. Since most of us went to the Center after school, I made little groups—three buddies with three younger kids. If that guy in the van even thought about coming up to a kid again, he wouldn't dare do it when they were with us older kids.*

The buddy system worked so good, we kept doing it for the rest of the school year, even after nobody had seen that van for months. That was probably why Dr. Johnson wrote a recommendation letter to help me get into the program at Ainsley. She kept saying, "You're a born leader, Caprice. This program sounds like it's right up your alley."

And it was.

The whole time I was at Ainsley, I kept thinking how much I wanted to tell her that she was right about Ainsley. And me. It was a perfect fit.

• • • • •

The next thing I know, I'm in the art room with a bunch of little kids, organizing a whole bunch of fuzzy material that's already cut into the shapes of different animals. And I'm sorting fluff and colored felt and ribbons into piles on an empty table.

"I hope you are all excited to get started," the art teacher, Olivia, says to everyone. Her eyes are wide and there's a singsong in her voice.

The kids are bouncing outta their seats.

Olivia gives me a bunch of booklets to hand out. "Caprice is going to give you a book of how the stuffed animals will look when they're done. Look through it and let us know which one you want."

As soon as the kids start looking through the booklets, the whole room is nothing but oohs and ahhs. The pictures are adorable. Bears, elephants, pigs, even sloths and raccoons. I kinda wanna make something, too.

So I do. As I help the kids make their animals and decorate them with buttons and bows and stuff, I make a cute little koala bear for me. I even give him a little red bow tie. Of course, I act like I'm just making this bear to show the kids how to do it, but as we leave the room for lunch, I'm loving that little bear like I'm six.

At lunch, I sit down next to Nicole and she immediately snatches the bear outta my arms. "Awww." She hugs it tight with her eyes closed. "Why didn't you make me one?"

I take it back. "Because you have Anthony."

"Oh yeah." That gets a smile on her face. "But still."

Miss Lisa starts calling us to line up for lunch. I'm hungry, but something doesn't smell all that good. Maybe I just got used to the lunch at Ainsley.

We get in line and Nicole leans close to me and plays with the beads on my new necklace. Then she says, "You-know-who was so bad in dance today. Abeni *has* to be regretting her decision to give her the lead."

"Shhh," I say quickly, looking around. Nobody is near us, especially Gina. Thank God. "Nicole, I keep telling you, you're not good at whispering."

"I don't care. It's true."

"Well, just keep being amazing, and Abeni will notice. Maybe you'll get the lead next time."

Nicole folds her arms in front of her. "Maybe I won't even be in the dance next time."

It's hard watching Nicole get on herself like this. I wish she would get the lead already. Just so she could be the star at least once.

"I'm serious, Caprice. I'm thinking about trying out to be one of the ball boys for Anthony's team. Well, ball girl. It'll be a lot more fun, and I'll get to see him more than just a couple times a week."

She's waiting for me to talk her outta it, but I don't. I just say, "You have less than a week before the festival, so stay focused."

She sighs hard. "Whatever."

A few minutes later, we sit back down at our table with a tray of chicken franks, potato wedges, and coleslaw. We both just stare at the food.

"You first," Nicole says.

I laugh. "Why me?"

"You like trying new things. I'm a scaredy-cat."

I bust out laughing. I've never heard her say something like that before.

A minute later Ayla and Gina sit down next to us with their food. Before we can say anything, Gina takes a big bite out of her frank. We all watch her chew and swallow and then take another bite.

I shrug and take a bite of my own chicken frank. Warm chicken juice squirts in my mouth. It's *not* terrible tasting. And I'm hungry.

Nicole is the last one to try hers, and she catches up to us fast. "You think they have more of these?" she asks, and we all crack up for no reason.

That just gets us all talking, and it feels like I was never away.

A few minutes later, Ayla is telling us about some scary movie she watched last night, and outta the corner of my eye, I see the boys at the next table throwing something in the air, back and forth.

It takes me a few seconds to see what it is. My koala!

I jump up and scream, "That's my bear!"

This boy, Hector, holds the bear by the neck. "You want him back?"

"Yes!"

His hands tighten around the bear's neck until he's strangling him.

"What's wrong with you?" I shout.

"I hate this thing," he yells back. Then he throws him to another boy, Kevon.

Now I'm off my chair and running over to get him back. Kevon throws him to Bobby, who holds my koala by the arm and shakes him hard.

"Why are you doing this?" I ask, trying to grab the bear outta Bobby's hand.

He raises his arm high above his head. Then he jumps up on his chair. "Why do you girls like these bears so much?" he asks, not to me really. It's like he's really talking to the other boys. "You wanna kiss it?" Then he actually starts hugging my bear and kissing it and acting like a total idiot. And of course, all the boys are laughing. "You girls like these things more than you like us guys."

He throws the bear down to the boys and it's caught by . . . Jarrett, who just got here. I put my hands on my hips. "It's mine, Jarrett. Give it back to me."

Jarrett reaches over to give it back to me, but before I can get it, Kevon grabs it from him.

"Bobby," Kevon says, "don't let Jarrett get it. He likes her."

Jarrett's eyes get big. He opens his mouth, but nothing comes out. Kevon is his brother, so everybody knows he's telling the truth.

Bobby is still on the chair with my bear again. I'm tired of this. I jump up on the chair next to him, elbow him in the ribs, and grab my bear back. It happens so fast, he never sees it coming. I point my finger in his face. "Don't mess with me, Bobby. My dad's a Marine."

I jump down. Okay, Dad isn't really a Marine anymore. Not technically. But he always says, "Once a Marine, always a Marine."

The girls are clapping, so I take a bow and I sit back down, rubbing my poor bear the whole time. "Can you believe he was jealous of a little bear?" I ask them. Then I speak louder and ask, "What, do they really think we would hug and kiss *them* if we didn't have stuffed animals?"

The girls laugh.

Sometimes I really don't understand boys at all.

The girls stay happy and united all through lunch, so when we're finished eating, I pull out the clipboard right there at the table. I tell everyone about Woman Group and how I need at least fifteen people to sign up. "We have to stick together," I tell them. "Why should the boys have Man Group and we get nothing?"

That works. I get five signatures, everyone at our table except Ayla, who started texting and isn't paying attention to any of us anymore. I'll have to get her to sign later. I even get a few more signatures from other tables.

I'm holding my bear tight as we walk outta the cafeteria, past those boys again. Jarrett holds the door for me. "Those guys," he starts. "Sorry for the way—"

"Thanks for trying to give me back my bear. Your friends are morons."

"Yeah, they know they are."

I shake my head.

"Did the flyers work?" he asks. "You get the girls to sign up?"

"I need five more."

Jarrett tells me good luck, and he heads toward the computer room while most everybody else goes outside. We have a break now, and it's not as crazy hot today.

Outside, some of the boys are dividing themselves up into teams for something. I stick my koala in my backpack so they don't try to steal him again and follow Gina, who decides to use the short ledge near the parking lot as a balance beam. She takes my hand and helps me find my balance, then she shows me how to do some really easy moves. Well, easy for her.

I look over to Nicole, who's sitting on a bench, and say, "Watch this." She's already looking at me, upset.

I do a very shaky arabesque, still holding Gina's hand. When I'm standing on my two feet again, she claps. But Nicole doesn't. When I look back over to her, she's not even paying attention.

I thank Gina for the gymnastics lesson and jump down. Nicole is already feeling bad about not getting the dance lead. Maybe this is making things worse.

Bobby comes over and grabs Ayla around the waist. She turns around, punches him in the arm, then chases him across the basketball court.

I sit next to Nicole. "It's too hot to run around," I say, watching Ayla catch Bobby and grab him the way he did to her. Only he likes it.

"It's too hot to do fake gymnastics, too," she says, not even looking at me.

"You're probably right." Sometimes I just don't wanna get into anything with her. Especially for something that's not important to me. Like this.

Outta the corner of my eye, I see Jarrett near the doorway, waving for me to come over. I get up and go over, trying not to bring attention to myself. Bad enough everyone knows he likes me.

"There's a bunch of girls in the computer room," he says. "Sixth graders."

"Ooh, thanks." I grab my backpack off the bench and follow him back there. Fast. Inside, there are four girls hard at work. Two girls are on the computer designing some kinda world outta a science fiction movie. One is on the floor sketching something, and the other one is creating storyboards.

Jarrett goes back to his movie music while I look at their project.

Everything is beautiful. I probably say "Wow" ten times. It's like they're creating their own world. "Is this a new role-playing game or something?" I ask Tandi, the only girl I know. She used to live across the street from me before I moved.

"Yeah," she says. "Wait till it's finished."

"You guys are so talented," I tell them. Even though the design on the computer and the drawings are just sketches, there's enough detail to get an idea what they're creating. It's cool. I'm so glad Jarrett told me about these girls. They'll be the youngest girls in Woman Group, but I wish I had a group like that when I was going into sixth grade. Might have made seventh grade much better.

I tell the girls what we're planning with Woman Group, and they sign up right away. I hang out with them for a little while, hearing more about their stories. There's something about them. They're so confident. I think I was that way, too, two years ago. Before everything changed.

I wonder if I'll ever get that back.

Actually, in a way, I kinda felt that confident at Ainsley. I felt sure of myself, like I was with girls who were like me, even when they were from halfway around the world. Of course, that didn't last. Friday night ruined that feeling.

Looking at these girls who are so focused on what they're creating, all I can think is, *I hope they stay this way.*

Jarrett leaves with me and we walk down the hall together. "Thanks to you, I only need one more signature." I know exactly who I have to get.

"You happy to be back here?"

"Yeah, really happy."

"What about next summer?" he asks. "You gonna go away again?"

I smile. "Did you miss me?" I say it kinda teasing. But kinda serious.

"No, um . . ." He looks so embarrassed. Cute.

"I'm kidding," I say. "Really." There's something kinda fun playing around with him. Just as long as everything stays like this. Easy.

I remember the night before I left for Ainsley. I was feeling everything. I was excited and nervous, but I was also sad. I felt like I was getting ripped away from everything—Mom, my friends, the Center. And even though I was looking forward to this whole new experience, I wasn't sure I was going away for the right reason. Like, was I doing this for me or to save my family? And was that even my job?

Sometimes when you're having a whole bunch of feelings at the same time, you end up not really feeling anything. That's what I was feeling that whole day. Nothing.

It was the Saturday before the Fourth of July, and we were having a block party that afternoon. We did it every year, like, to start the summer off right. There was a DJ playing music, and the street in front of the Center was closed to traffic so we could dance and jump double dutch and play all kinds of games in the middle of the street all day. There was lots and lots of food and ice cream. It was great.

At night, the street was full of people hanging out, listening to music, sitting on folding chairs and their cars. There were cheeseburgers and corn on the cob and fried dough. Every few minutes somebody would throw a firecracker. It was loud and crazy out there, and I loved all of it.

But still, it felt like I was watching everybody have fun, not having fun myself. I just couldn't get outta my head. I wanted to take it all in, because it felt like I was gonna miss my whole summer. I wouldn't be back for seven weeks. I think I wanted something to remember when I was gone.

While Nicole and most of the girls were on the sidewalk looking at their phones and copying some dance, I sat on the curb watching them. It was still pretty hot outside, even at 7:30, too hot to feel like dancing with them.

Anyway, I was too busy thinking of Ainsley, which I had only seen in pictures. What would it be like to be somewhere else for so long? What would I be like in a different place?

Would I be the same person? Or would I change, too?

That was the kinda thing I was thinking when Jarrett came over to me. The boys had done a step routine for everyone earlier. "I thought you left or something," he said. He was eating a red, white, and blue Popsicle. "You want one?"

"No, I'm okay," I said, trying to lift my voice so I sounded natural.

"Are you busy? I mean—"

"No, no. I'm just, I don't know, like, trying to remember everything for when I'm away."

Jarrett sat down on the curb next to me. "I thought you were only going away for a couple of weeks."

"No. Seven." I laughed a little.

"Seven weeks?" He looked kinda stunned. "Um, that's the whole summer practically."

He was right. I was going away for a long time.

"You scared?" he asked, and he looked me in the eye, which made me feel a little uncomfortable. "Because it's okay to be scared. I would be . . . I mean, not scared, but—"

I giggled. "It's okay to admit you would be scared, Jarrett."

He just looked down and licked his Popsicle, which was melting all over his hand.

So I admitted, "Yeah, I'm scared. Nervous. It's gonna be weird not being here every day. Are you gonna make a new movie trailer this summer without me?"

"I don't know. Ennis wants to make a funny cartoon."

"That'll be cool. I'll be back in time for the festival, so I hope it's ready."

"It will be." We looked at each other again, both of us smiling. And even though we were surrounded by a whole block of people and there was music and laughing, all of that kinda faded away and it was just me and Jarrett. I'd never felt that, whatever it was, with anyone. I don't know. It felt like we were connected.

Just then a huge green-and-yellow firework boomed, and whatever it was between us was gone. We both looked up as the colors zigzagged down from the sky. Then, when I looked over at Jarrett again, his head was down and he was licking his Popsicle. I wanted to say something, but I didn't know what.

Again, I was having too many feelings to know what to do with them. It was too much. Jarrett and I had a few seconds where I felt really close to him, where it felt like just me and him. It didn't last long, and all I could feel was relieved. Those kinda feelings were too much for me. I wasn't ready.

So I jumped up and said, "Uh, I better get home before, you know . . . I need to finish packing."

Jarrett mumbled something about me having fun this summer and I told him, "You, too."

I walked away from him without looking back. I didn't know what all my feelings meant. It was too much to deal with on my last night in Newark.

Luckily, I knew I wouldn't have to see Jarrett for seven weeks. Suddenly, that didn't seem like all that long. But maybe it would be enough time to know if I liked him or not.

When I get back outside, almost everyone is gone. Nicole is still there, eating sunflower seeds with Ayla. "Oh good, you're back," Nicole says to me, jumping up. "I was waiting for you. We need to get to the gym."

"What for?"

"You'll see," Ayla says.

Nicole giggles and adds, "It's new. For the summer. You'll like it."

Nicole and Ayla fly down the hall with me trying to keep up with them. Last summer we used to have photography after lunch. I guess things have changed.

"Wait," I say, and stop walking right outside the gym. They stop, too. "I have to get one more signature first. I have to turn this sheet in."

"You can do it later," Nicole says.

But I don't wanna wait. "Ayla, can you sign? It's for Woman Group." I try to take the pleading out of my voice, but I need her. I'm running out of girls to ask.

She waves her hand in my direction and goes, "I'll think about it." Then she hurries into the gym.

I roll my eyes and Nicole laughs. She hooks her arm around mine. "It's not her fault. There are boys in archery, so she *can't* be late."

I'm not sure I heard her right. "Archery? They're letting boys play with *arrows*?" This can't be true.

Nicole laughs. "I know, right? Sounds crazy, but don't worry about it. We had to learn everything about safety and all that."

"But—"

"Oh yeah, *Jarrett's* in the class." She smirks when she says this.

Part of me just wants to stay focused. I wanna get one more girl to sign and turn this in before something goes wrong. I don't want anything to mess this up for me.

But I let Nicole pull me into the gym, and I feel myself start to let go of everything. "But seriously," I say one more time. "They're giving the boys *real* arrows with sharp points?"

Nicole laughs. And so do I. I love when I let her happiness change me. It feels good. Even if it's just temporary.

Turns out, I'm pretty terrible at archery. But the other girls are fantastic! And since we play girls against the boys, we win easily. Of course, we spend extra time high-fiving each other.

I'm so happy I almost forget about the sign-up sheet. Until Ayla comes up to me. She's smiling, pumped from our win.

"I'm ready to sign," she says coolly, like she's doing me a favor. "Your group won't be any fun without me anyway."

I try to hide my smile while I hand her the clipboard and a pen, but I'm relieved. The girls are gonna have our own group. And yeah, it probably would be more fun without Ayla, but I don't have a choice.

She hands me back the clipboard, and I tell her thanks. I look over the sheet again, just to make sure I have fifteen names. And I do.

I did it.

I practically run upstairs with the clipboard, hoping it's not too late, that Mrs. Prajapati isn't already gone for the day, but she's not. She's in her office, still working on her computer.

I don't really wanna bother her, but I knock on the open door anyway.

"Caprice, come in."

I hold up the clipboard. "It's done!"

She laughs. "I had no doubt you could do it."

I hand her the sign-up sheet and stand there on the other side of her desk while she scans through the signatures. "So, we're going to have a Woman Group," she says. "This really means a lot to you, doesn't it?"

She says it casually, and it's not really what she says but how she looks at me that feels like a piece of glass in my heart. It cuts me. But I don't want her to see. So I just say, "No. I mean, kinda. Yeah, it does. Girls have a lot of stuff going on. Everything. It's the girls . . . we have more stuff to deal with than the boys."

Things happen to girls.

I stop talking and stand there, feeling cut again. I have to take a couple of deep breaths to stop hurting.

It's hard though.

"You really *need* this group." It's like she's realizing this for the first time, and now she's got a worried look on her face, something she's never directed toward me before. She's never needed to.

I stand there, not able to breathe. I open my mouth to try to suck in some air, but I can't catch a full breath. I gasp again. And again. Then I cover my mouth so Mrs. Prajapati won't notice, so she won't know there's something wrong with me.

But it's too late.

"Caprice, are you okay?" Mrs. Prajapati stands up and comes around her desk.

I nod, but I still can't talk. The tears and the sobs come so fast, I feel weak.

That's when she wraps her arms around me. Tight. And she's saying the right things, too.

She tells me it's okay, that sometimes things feel like it's too much, but right now I'm just standing here in her office, and right here everything is alright. She tells me all I have to do at this moment is breathe. That's it. Breathe.

Finally, I tell her I'm okay, and she lets me go. But she's still looking at me like I'm gonna fall apart again.

"Is everything okay at home, Caprice?" she asks. "Are you safe? Is there a reason I should be worried about you?"

I shake my head and tell her no, that everything at home is fine. But then it happens again. The gasping for air, the hug, the *just breathe and everything is going to be okay.* This time, I let her hold me a little longer, just to be sure.

I wanna believe her. I do.

∙ ∙ ◆ ∙ ∙

"Look what came today," Mom says as I come through the front door. She's working at her little desk in the living room. "It's over there." She points to the other side of the room.

"What is it?" I'm not sure what she's pointing to exactly. I turn around and see that she's pointing to the little table where she keeps her keys and the mail.

"The package," she says. "It's from Ainsley. Not only that, but the resident coordinator, Ms. Lu, called me this morning just to make sure we knew what you need to bring with you. She said not to worry about notebooks and school supplies because you can get all of that at the campus bookstore. I have to order your uniforms though."

"Oh yeah." How could I forget about that?

The Ainsley girls have to wear uniforms for school. Terra has a bunch of them in her closet, and one day I tried one on, just to see what I'd look like as an official Ainsley girl. Their uniform is actually kinda cute. Solid navy pleated skirt, gray blazer, white blouse. No tie. No plaid. I liked the way I looked and *felt* wearing it.

"Even if I order the uniforms now, they won't be there in time for the first day of school," Mom continues. "But they have some donated uniforms you can borrow in the meantime. Of course, I can't order anything until after you call Dr. Suzanne to let her know you'd like to accept her offer."

I pick up the large envelope. There's something about the fancy Ainsley International logo on the front that makes me feel kinda intimidated. It's like too much for me.

"Ms. Lu also said the girls have to dress for dinner. You can stay in your uniform or change into a dress or a skirt and blouse. So we need to get you some new things. You're allowed to wear whatever you want on the weekends."

It was kinda like that for the summer program, too. We had to change into a dress or skirt for dinner and look "presentable" as Dr. Suzanne told us during orientation. I'd only brought two dresses with me, but Terra had a bunch of presentable clothes in her closet, and she let me wear them all the time.

The Ainsley envelope is opened already, so I just slip out the huge softcover book. It's beautiful.

AINSLEY INTERNATIONAL
STUDENT HANDBOOK

On the cover, there are pictures of girls doing all kinds of things: sitting in class and studying in the library, hanging out in their dorm and the cafeteria, playing field hockey and volleyball, swimming, rowing, painting. There are even photos of Ainsley girls on trips to other countries, in groups in front of the Eiffel Tower, someplace that looks like the rain forest, and some big castle somewhere, maybe England.

No matter what they're doing, everyone looks happy.

I flip through the book. There's a colorful map of the campus on the inside cover. I can't help but smile when I see the pond and the library and my dorm. And the paths leading from one building to the other. In just seven weeks, I have so many memories.

"That book is beautiful, isn't it?" Mom says. "I feel like I'm sending you off to college."

I close the book. "There's a lot to do," I say. "Like, before I leave."

"I'm working on a master list of things we need to do and buy. It's okay if you don't have everything like winter clothes and boots, because we can get all of that when I visit."

"You're gonna visit?"

"Of course!" Mom gets up and grabs me up from behind. "I'm gonna miss my baby." She kisses me on the cheek and laughs.

"Mom! I'm not a baby!"

"Don't start that with me."

I sigh extra long and extra hard, just for dramatic purposes.

Mom walks into the kitchen and I follow her. She takes a frozen vegetable lasagna outta the freezer and preheats the oven, then me and her sit at the table and flip through the Ainsley book together.

"This is my favorite spot on campus," I say, pointing to the picture of the little gazebo behind the Arts Center. "I love all the flowerpots that are hanging inside. I took a lot of pictures here." Then, as we turn the pages, I tell her all about our scavenger hunt, and point to the huge fountain in front of the main building, which solved the riddle about finding the oldest thing on campus. "We had to jump into the fountain before the other team got there, to get the key that was left there. Then we had to try to figure out what door that key fit, soaking wet. It was so much fun!"

Mom says, "I feel like you've had all these new experiences I wasn't there for."

"We talked all the time!"

"I know, but when you go back, you're going to grow up and do all these interesting things, and I'm going to miss them all. I'll just hear about them after the fact. That's not the same thing." She puts her hand on mine.

"I'll try to grow real slow," I say, grinning.

The phone rings and I jump. And it's hard to ignore the look she gives me, more surprised than worried. "Everything okay?"

"Huh? Oh, yeah." My heart is racing.

She gets up to answer the phone and I put my head down, holding my breath.

Please don't be Mrs. Prajapati. Please don't be Mrs. Prajapati.

"Perfect timing," Mom says into the phone. "I was just missing you."

It's Dad.

I exhale.

I sit quietly while they talk, looking over the list Mom made and thinking about everything I have to do if I'm really leaving in five days.

"Here." Mom hands me the phone. "Dad wants to talk to you."

This feels like all of last year when Dad was away, when we only got to talk on the phone.

Dad and I talk for a few minutes. I tell him about archery, and Woman Group starting this week, and he tells me he'll be here Sunday to drive me back up to Ainsley. "Make sure you're packed and ready to go," he says. "Because I don't want to—"

"I know, I know," I say. "Hit traffic!" Even Dad has to laugh. "I'll be ready," I tell him.

"Your father is so predictable," Mom says, putting the lasagna in the oven. "Don't tell him I said that."

On the phone, Dad says, "Tell her I heard that."

"He heard that," I say, and Mom laughs.

After I finish talking to Dad, I give the phone back to Mom so they can keep talking. I grab the Ainsley book and go down the hall to my room. They probably wanna talk without me around.

They both seem like they're in a good mood. I hope they stay that way and don't start arguing about Mom's family again.

baltimore

baltimore was dark with wet streets.
it was wind.
it was the slap of bare feet
on hard concrete.
baltimore was being scared and cold.
so, so cold.
it was helicopters
and police lights
and white hospital halls.
baltimore was loud screams
and angry voices
and crying.
my crying.

After dinner, when I'm back in my room, I get a text from Deja.

> terra says ur coming back. t? f?

I don't know how to answer. It's not true *or* false.
I text back:

> more t than f. but not 100%

> whats the prob?

> dr. s wants me to call her to make it official

> call her then

> i will, miss bossy pants!

> who me???

> what are u & kimberly doing? does she like 🍁?

> she loves all the trini food my grandma is feeding her!

> 😊

One day at Ainsley, Deja got a care package from her grandmother. It was a tin of homemade ginger cookies wrapped in bubble wrap. I forgot what Deja called them, but they were crunchy and delicious. We sat in the hallway, me, Deja, and Kimberly, and ate half the tin while popping the bubble wrap and laughing. I think that was the first day I felt like I belonged there.

I look down at my phone, where Deja's written:

come back caprice we can be partners again!

That's when I get this tingly feeling in my stomach. The good kind of tingly. Deja and I worked together really great this summer. It would be fun to be partners with her again, to be in class with her, and down the hall from her in our dorm. We would have so much fun.

But then I wouldn't be here. I'd miss my last year of middle school.

I can't think of what to text Deja. I don't want her thinking I don't wanna be partners again, because I do. But me and Nicole have been class partners for almost forever.

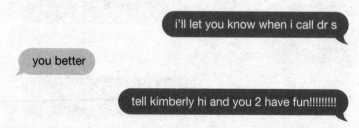

i'll let you know when i call dr s

you better

tell kimberly hi and you 2 have fun!!!!!!!!!

I put the phone on the charger and pick up *Breath, Eyes, Memory.* I read until I can't keep my eyes open.

I remember making lasagna with Grandma. Sometimes she would let me help her lay out the lasagna and the meat sauce and the cheese in the pan in neat rows. One day, while the food was in the oven, I went down to the basement to see what Uncle Raymond was doing.

His room was on one side of the basement, the side by the window. Uncle Raymond always kept his side of the basement clean because he was gonna be an army soldier, and they had to be perfect.

I remember he was playing a video game, so I stayed and watched. Then he told me about the army, that he would learn everything about self-defense.

He paused the game and stood up. "Try to attack me," he said. He started to walk away and I sneaked up behind him. Then I jumped up and grabbed him around the waist. I tried to wrap my legs around his thighs, but he spun me off of him so fast I landed on the rug in front of him.

"See," he said. "You gotta be prepared for anything when you're in the army."

I remember lying there for a few seconds, the sting of hitting the floor still vibrating through my body. It hurt, but I didn't wanna cry. I wanted to be a strong army girl.

So I tried again. I ran up on him again, and this time he dropped me on the bed. It didn't hurt. It all happened so fast, it made me laugh.

Raymond grabbed me up and dropped me again on his bed. Over and over.

That's when we heard the basement door open and Grandma start to come downstairs. The smell of the food cooking in the oven followed her down the stairs.

But first, without saying anything, me and Uncle Raymond scrambled into place next to each other on the bed, in front of the TV. He unpaused the video game and went back to shooting the zombies that were coming from every direction. When he shot them, there was a squishing noise as their brains oozed out of their heads. It was disgusting. Scary.

I hid my face under the pillow, but I kept popping out because I wanted to see it. But I didn't, at the same time.

I was four.

Back then, I liked giggling and screaming and giggling some more. It felt exciting that he was letting me watch him. Like I was doing something only grown-ups were supposed to be doing.

Grandma started putting the dirty clothes in the washing machine. "If you don't stop giving that kid nightmares . . ." she told Uncle Raymond.

"It's just a game, Ma," he said. "Caprice knows that. She's not stupid."

"She's not the stupid one," Grandma said. She was always saying stuff like that to Uncle Raymond. It made me feel sorry for him.

That was when Uncle Raymond paused the game again and grabbed my feet. Before I could pull away, he was tickling them and I was wiggling around on his bed, laughing so hard I couldn't catch my breath. "Yo, Ma," he said. "She's only ticklish on one foot! It's crazy!"

"If you don't leave that little girl alone, I will . . ." Grandma stopped talking and moved away from the washing machine. "Raymond, is that a . . . ?"

"What?"

Grandma was pointing to the space between the washing machine and the dryer. "Is that a mouse? Oh, Lord."

Raymond got up, went over to her, and took a look. "Yep, it's a baby mouse. They come in the basement sometimes. I hear them at night. That's why I put down those traps."

"Get rid of it," Grandma said, moving farther away from the washing machine.

"You want to see it, Caprice?" Uncle Raymond asked me. "It's dead. It can't hurt you."

Again, I was scared and curious and excited all at the same time. And that's probably why I remember it. I wanted to see it, but I was afraid. But I didn't want him to know. So I walked closer, even as Grandma told me over and over to stay away and not listen to that boy.

I had to see.

I moved as slow as possible over to Uncle Raymond, where he was now holding the white sticky trap. On top was a small mouse with its fur stuck to the glue. My heart was racing, that's how scared I was.

Once I saw it, I screamed and ran over to Grandma and wrapped my arms around her waist and buried my face in her stomach. "I told you not to look at that thing," she said. "Don't come to me when you have a nightmare tonight."

She picked me up and carried me back upstairs where there weren't any mice, dead or alive. In that moment, I hated Uncle Raymond. He shouldn't have shown me that mouse. Or those zombies. I wasn't a grown-up. I was just a little kid.

$\bullet \cdot \bullet \cdot \bullet$

In the locker room on our trip to the pool the next day, nothing about me is good enough for Nicole. My one-piece bathing suit is too *basic* even though I wore it all the time at Ainsley, no problem.

"Here, I brought this for you," she says, pulling a fuchsia bikini top from her backpack. "This'll look nice with your skin color." She holds it out to me like she really thinks I'm gonna take it.

I fold my arms. "I'm not wearing a bikini, Nicole. You know that."

"It's just the top. It comes with boy shorts." She pulls the shorts out of her bag. They're black with fuchsia trim. "Here." She hands both of them to me.

"Why do you always do this?" I ask her. "Why do you always make me feel—"

"It's not that serious, Caprice," she says. "It's a bathing suit. I mean, we're going into eighth grade and you're still dressing like we're in fourth."

"What if I don't wanna wear this?"

"Whatever then. Don't blame me for trying to help you."

"You're not helping me. You're—"

"Don't you wanna look good? Don't you want a boyfriend?"

"Oh, so this is about a boyfriend?"

"Yeah. No." Nicole looks completely frustrated by a normal question. "It's not only about that. You're cute, Caprice. Why do you always hide your body? We're at the pool!"

"Fine!" I take the bathing suit from her and go into the changing room to put it on. It's not that bad. The color is pretty, and at least the shorts cover my butt.

But all the while, as we put our clothes in lockers and walk outta the locker room carrying our towels, I'm mad inside. Not mad at Nicole as much as I'm mad at myself. For doing what she wants, as usual.

my body

it is changing.
i have a waist and breasts and even hips now
but my body isn't anything special.
i'm just one of the girls in the middle
between the skinny girls and the curvy girls.
i don't stand out.
sometimes i wonder,
is there something on my body i can't see?
something that only boys can see?
and men?
that lets them know
i've already been touched.

＊＊＊＊＊

Because there's no way I'm gonna walk to the pool with these little shorts on, I wrap my towel around my waist and I don't even care that Nicole is giving me all kinda side eye. I know what she's thinking, that she doesn't know why I can't act my age. Why do I have to cover up? Why can't I just be comfortable with the fact that boys are gonna look at me? But whatever. She got me to wear this bathing suit. That's all I'm giving her today.

The Center picked the perfect day for a trip to the pool. It's sticky hot. If they didn't bring us here, we would have had to stay inside the building all day, like when it rains. And those days are always the most boring.

As we get closer to the pool, we pass by these two boys from our grade who I haven't seen since school got out. They're not here with the Center like most of the other kids. They don't say anything to us. They just stand there, which is a good thing. But about two seconds later, I hear Frankie whisper, "She's a B-plus now. Nicole, she's still an A."

"Definitely," the other boy, Sheldon, says. "More like an A-plus." And they both laugh.

My mouth flies open and before I can stop myself, I'm spinning around. Nicole grabs my arm and says, "It's nothing. They're stupid."

But I'm not Nicole. And I don't care how stupid they are. You don't have to be smart to respect girls. I can feel my face getting hot. I wanna tell these boys what I should have told those men in the parking lot.

"What's the matter with you?" I yell. Then I shake Nicole's

hand off my arm and practically run back over to where Frankie and Sheldon are standing, trying to look cool, like they're not two losers with nothing better to do but stand there judging girls.

Of course, they don't say anything.

"What?" I scream. "*You're* so perfect? Who are you to grade us? How would you feel if girls started grading you?"

"I would give you both an F-minus!" Nicole screams. All of a sudden, she's involved, too.

Frankie raises his hands. "Calm down!"

Something about the way he says it, with a smile on his face, makes me even madder. He's treating us like we're weird for getting mad when they're the ones who started it.

"I'm not gonna calm down," I yell back even though I'm like a foot away from him now. "Admit you're wrong and apologize."

The boys look at each other and laugh.

It's the laugh that makes me furious. "What's so funny?"

Frankie opens then closes his mouth—and I have to say, he actually looks a little nervous. Good.

"Apologize," I say again.

"What are you mad for?" Sheldon asks. "Y'all got good grades."

"Apologize!" This time I scream so loud Sheldon actually jumps.

"Okay, okay," he says. "Sorry. God." He walks away, leaving Frankie standing there.

"Look," Frankie says. "You don't have to scream. I have a weak eardrum and . . ." He stops lying, and we just stare at each other until he says, "Sorry, okay?"

"Was that so hard?" I ask. "You could have done that five minutes ago."

"I did it, so stop talking to me." Frankie walks away, too.

That's when Nicole starts laughing. "You're unbelievable," she tells me. "But that was amazing."

I feel my face and my whole body start to relax. Cool down. And finally, I'm smiling. "I can't believe they gave me a B-plus," I say. "I've never gotten anything less than an A-minus in my whole life!"

"There's something wrong with you," Nicole says. "Seriously."

We walk toward the pool, laughing.

• • • • •

An hour later, all of us kids from the Center have taken over the pool. We're not swimming or anything, just playing around. The boys and Gina are jumping into the pool over and over, completely ignoring the lifeguard, who keeps telling them to stop. Every time they jump in, we all scream because of the splash. It's crazy.

When I was at Ainsley, this is what I missed about summer in Newark. This right here.

But for some reason, I'm having a hard time keeping my mind here. It's like what happened at the party on Friday. I was having a good time, but something inside was pulling me down.

I can't let that happen again. Not here.

I pull myself outta the pool. "Where are you going?" Nicole asks, raising her voice over everything going on around us.

I stand there by the pool dripping. "I, um, I'll be back."

I run over to the chair where I left my towel. I wipe my face, then wrap the towel tight around me. My heart is racing and I don't know why. Everything is fine.

I'm fine.

I sit down and remember what I tried to do on Friday. *Breathe.* It didn't work then, though. I couldn't do it.

I remember running to the lake, trying not to cry, trying to get out from under the darkness of all those trees. My body felt like it was spinning. I needed a place to stop. I needed to feel safe.

As I ran, I felt the sticks under my feet, heard the cracking they made as I pounded over them. Then there was the clearing and the other kids, all laughing and having the best time with each other. I wasn't alone anymore.

Terra was there, talking to some girls from the swim team. I stopped running. I had to calm down at least long enough to get to Terra.

I had to breathe. Just breathe.

"You okay?"

I look up and see Nicole standing over me. I don't know how long she's been there.

"Huh? Oh, yeah." I rub my side. "I think I got a cramp or something."

She sits on the chair with me. "Bobby made up a new game. It's like freeze tag but you have to stay frozen underwater."

I smile weakly. "He's always making up stuff."

"You gonna come back?"

"Uh, yeah. Give me a few minutes."

She doesn't move.

"I'm okay," I say again. "I'm just . . ."

We're silent for a long minute. Then she puts her arm around my waist. "Is something wrong? You can tell me anything."

"I'm fine." I probably say this too fast.

Nicole sighs like she's giving up on me and stands up. "Okay. Don't take too long." She runs back to the pool and climbs down the ladder. A few seconds later, she's back in the middle of everyone, laughing.

I used to be able to do that. Now I'm not so sure I can anymore.

What's wrong with me?

I sit there on the chair for probably another fifteen minutes, just breathing.

This isn't Friday. It's not the party. I'm stronger now.

Slowly, I stand up and throw the towel back on the chair. I'm here. This is fun. I'm having fun.

I run back over to the pool and make myself jump in.

•• •• •• ••

I remember Friday, my last night at Ainsley. About a half hour after I hung up from talking to Mom, I was still sitting on my bed, trying to figure out what was going on with me. Why did it feel like I'd had an earthquake inside of me all of a sudden?

Terra came back to the room with something wrapped in a napkin. "Here's something to get the party started," she said, smiling like she was doing something so wrong.

She'd been at the gym helping to set up for the party. Terra was always involved with everything. She'd even created some of the decorations.

Terra sat on the bed next to me and opened the napkin. Chocolate chip cookies.

"Did you steal these?" I asked, reaching for one.

"Kind of. I was in charge of putting all the snacks out."

I laughed out loud. "You?"

"I know. Their mistake. Anyway, I didn't steal them. I consider it payment for all the hard work I did."

I bit into my cookie, which was crispy with melty chocolate chips. "Oh my God."

"Worth stealing, right?"

I nodded.

"Well, there'll be three trays of them at the party. Plus the best caramel popcorn you can think of. I tried to smuggle some of that out, too, but Mrs. Finnegan was hanging around that table. I think she knew I was up to something sinister."

I laughed and took another bite.

For a little while, me and her munched without talking, and my mind slipped back to Grandma and Baltimore and everything else I never really thought about anymore.

Tried not to think about.

"You okay?" Terra asked. "You look . . . Did something happen?"

"No, not really. I talked to my mom."

"Everything alright at home?"

I shrugged. "Nobody's home. My parents are flying to Syracuse from Detroit. They'll be here in the morning." I grabbed another cookie and so did Terra.

Finally, when we'd both had three cookies, Terra jumped up. "Time to get ready. Did you figure out what you're wearing? I hope you're not wearing that."

I had on shorts and an MIT T-shirt. "Of course not!" I said.

"Good. Because the boys will be here in an hour and—" She looked at her phone. "An hour and twelve minutes!"

Terra wasn't really all that boy crazy or anything, but having boys around was rare at Ainsley. All the Ainsley girls were practically giddy when they talked about how the boys were coming there for the party.

Which was weird, because we went on the college trip with the boys from Kentworth and spent the whole day with them while we got tours of Harvard and MIT. And yeah, the boys were fun and everything, but I didn't see why everyone was losing their minds over them. I mean, they were just regular boys.

I stood up, and surprisingly, I didn't feel dizzy. Maybe it had passed, whatever it was that had hit me. I took a deep breath. I was going to be okay.

"Do you think Isaiah is going to be here?" Terra asked.

I shrugged. "Probably. Remember how he was dancing to the music in that student center at Harvard. Or was that MIT?" The schools were blended together in my mind.

"You excited to see him?"

"Not really. We just hung out on the trip. It's not like we're a couple or anything."

"Do you like him?"

I shrugged. "He's cool." I didn't know what Terra wanted me to say, or how she wanted me to act. Was I supposed to jump up and down because a boy who was kinda becoming a friend might be coming to Ainsley? I wasn't feeling that way about him. Not even close.

Still, he was a nice guy. We'd sat across the aisle from each other on the bus ride to Boston, and he was funny. A couple of hours into our trip, he secretly blew up a huge beach ball without any of the adults on the bus noticing. Then we all bounced the ball around the bus, watching it hit the roof and the tops of other kids' heads, all of us laughing so loud . . . until the ball got confiscated by one of the Kentworth teachers, who turned to Isaiah right away and said, "We will discuss this matter later, Mr. Brooks."

"Why are you blaming me?" Isaiah asked, eyes wide, like he was so innocent. But a second later, a smile escaped his lips, giving away his guilt. "Okay, Mr. Atkins," he said. "I look forward to our discussion and your usual understanding nature, of course."

When the teacher went back to the front of the bus, I whispered to Isaiah across the aisle, "Are you gonna be in trouble?"

"Yeah, probably. But it was worth it. This bus ride is long!" We'd both laughed.

Before the party, I thought it would be nice to see him again. At least I knew I would have some laughs that night.

But of course I didn't tell that to Terra. I didn't want her to make more outta it than I was.

"I'm going to wear my white jeans and this red top I haven't worn yet," I said. "It's really cute. What about you?"

"I have a blue summer dress with little white flowers. I've been waiting for the right time to wear it."

"It's my last night," I said, and it was starting to feel like the end. "But I'm not gone yet!" I smiled and tried my hardest to be happy.

I decided right there. I wasn't going to think about anything that night, nothing except having fun. I was going to have a good time.

· · · · ·

I hear music playing as I climb my outside steps, and by the time I get to the front door, I can hear laughing and an En Vogue song playing. Lana must be visiting.

They're still talking when I come inside. I hear Lana say, "So what's the deal? You going back to Detroit?"

"Not sure yet," Mom says. "I want Caprice to make the decision on her own."

"So you wait?"

"Looks that way."

I shut the door behind me, loudly, so they'll know I'm home. I step into the living room and say hi to Mom and Lana.

"You're home early," Mom says. "We were just talking about you."

I heard.

I drop my backpack, and Lana stands up to give me a hug. While she's doing it, she pulls my locs outta the ponytail holder. "You need to wash this hair tonight. That chlorine will—"

"I know," I say. "I'm on it."

Lana raises one eyebrow at me. "Oh, I forgot. You're grown now. You can take care of yourself, right, Miss Boarding School?"

Mom laughs.

"I'm just saying, I know what to do." I turn to Mom. "Why were you talking about me?"

"Lana was just wondering if you made your decision yet. Don't forget, you have to call Dr. Suzanne this week. Don't wait till the last minute."

"I won't."

The phone rings again, and I can't tell if Mom's talking to someone from the hospital or her family because she sounds the same with all of them. She's formal and detached, like she's not talking about her own mother. I just hope everything is okay.

• • • • •

Lana can't stay for dinner, so it's just Mom and me again. Mom's distracted. She's off the phone, but I can tell something's wrong by the way she's just kind of staring off into space.

"Is it Grandma?" I ask quietly.

She nods. "They say she's getting worse. Nothing's working."

I wanna know what she's planning to do, but I don't wanna hear the answer.

After a while Mom says, "The thing is, I didn't know anything about all these health problems she was having. You know? She's been going through a lot for a long time, but . . ." She shrugs.

"It's not your fault," I say, even though I know that's not what she's saying.

"It's just such a shame. When I was your age, I wished I had a close relationship with my mother. But it never happened. We were never on the same wavelength, you know? We were polite and kind to each other, but there wasn't a bond. I always said, if I ever had a daughter, she and I would be close. There would be trust."

"There is," I tell her. "We have all that. Nothing's ever gonna change."

"Let's make sure we keep it that way," Mom says. "Because if anything ever happened between us, I—"

"Don't worry," I tell her. "It won't."

"I don't want you to think that when you're away we're not going to be as close, because I want us to be in touch all the time. Every day. Twice a day. Three times—"

"Okay, okay!" I laugh. "I get it!"

Mom gets up and gives me a quick hug. "I love you so much, baby." She kisses the top of my head.

"I love you, too."

Mom starts to clear the table of the dinner dishes. So I ask what I've been trying not to. "You're not gonna have to go to Baltimore, are you?"

"Aunt Gwen is trying to reach Uncle Raymond. He's stationed in Germany. Hopefully, he'll be able to come home and deal with this." She shakes her head sadly. "Your grandma probably wouldn't want me making decisions for her health anyway."

All I hear is, *Uncle Raymond is coming home.*

My brain starts racing. If we end up going to Baltimore, we might be there the same time he is. Where would we stay if we go back there? Grandma's house? Aunt Gwen's house? A hotel? Where would *he* stay?

I have to plan.

Maybe I can ask Mom if I can stay with Nicole. Or Lana. Maybe *she* can bring me back to Ainsley. I have other options besides going to Baltimore. Dad wouldn't want me going back there anyway. He wouldn't let me go back no matter what.

"What's going on?" Mom asks. "You just checked out on me."

Now Mom sounds like Nicole. "I'm fine," I say.

"You're not getting all moody and *teenage* on me, are you? Because I thought I had until December for that."

Even though I'm thinking, *Mom and I won't be together for my birthday,* I make myself smile. "Why do you say *teenage* like it's a bad word? I'm not gonna change just because I turn thirteen."

"Famous last words!" Mom laughs. "I'm going to hold you to that!"

While Mom washes the dishes, I put away the leftovers and wipe down the table. She's right. I do feel kinda checked out tonight.

Mom comes up behind me and rubs my back. "Did you have a good time at the pool?"

"Yeah, we had fun. Well, I *did* have to tell some boys off. They were giving the girls *grades* for their bodies."

Mom gasps.

"I know, right? Don't worry. I shamed them. And forced them to apologize."

"That's my girl!"

I give Mom a hug and tell her I'm gonna go to bed early. But even as I walk down the hallway, I know going to bed doesn't mean going to sleep. My brain is all over the place. I don't know how I'm gonna turn it off.

I remember when Uncle Raymond used to wake me up. It would be late at night when Grandma was already sleeping. So it was just me and him awake with the whole house to ourselves.

I remember feeling tired, sleepy, and not really wanting to get out of bed, especially when my bed was warm and it was kinda cold in the house. But Uncle Raymond wanted to play with me, and I wanted to show him that I was a big girl, not a baby. I could stay up late, too.

Sometimes Uncle Raymond would have a surprise for me. A surprise party. I had to go with him to find out.

Uncle Raymond would press his finger to his lips as we tiptoed past Grandma's bedroom. If she heard us, she would get mad at Uncle Raymond for waking me up. And mad at me for getting outta bed. She would say I should know better.

But Grandma didn't know about our surprise parties. They didn't happen all the time. Only sometimes. I never knew when Uncle Raymond would plan something, and he never told me until we got down to the basement. He said that was what the word surprise meant.

Surprise parties could be anything. A surprise birthday party, just for me. A surprise Christmas, with Grandma's Christmas tree set up in the basement, with my favorite ornaments on it. The baby Jesus and Minnie Mouse, and even the angel on top. One time Uncle Raymond gave me a surprise Easter. He gave me a little stuffed bunny and jelly beans.

I never knew what it was gonna be. If it was gonna be a surprise. So I would quietly follow Uncle Raymond downstairs. All the way down to the basement.

I sit up in bed and gasp for breath over and over.

I wasn't dreaming. I'm still awake. But I'm remembering too much, and my heart is beating hard. Too hard. My whole body is like a heartbeat. Pounding.

I'm scared.

I get outta bed and walk around my tiny room. It's too small in here and the round window is too high. I feel trapped all of a sudden.

I walk out into the hall, not sure if I'm headed for the living room or Mom's room. But then I see the light is on in her room and the TV is on real low, so I knock.

"Caprice? You're up? Come in."

I go inside. It's just the light from the TV that's on. Mom is under her covers, but she sits up when I come in the room. "What's wrong, sweetie? You alright?"

"I had a nightmare." It's not true, and I sound like a four-year-old. But that's how I feel right now, standing there in the doorway.

Mom pulls the covers back from Dad's side of the bed. "Come and sleep with your mama, baby." She pats the empty space. "This will be fun."

I go over and climb into bed next to her. She slips her arm around my shoulders and kisses me on the cheek. "Bad nightmare?" she asks.

"No," I say. "I mean, I'm not sure. I don't really remember it. Just . . ." I shake my head. "It's gone."

"Yeah, I know that feeling. It's like your brain doesn't want you to remember."

I nod.

Mom turns off the TV, and in the darkness, she moves closer to me. "Go back to sleep," she whispers. "Any monsters come in here, don't worry. I'll protect you."

I snuggle into the pillow and inhale Dad's scent, which immediately starts to calm me down. I wanna go to sleep and not think anymore. And not remember. That's what I want. To stop remembering.

remembering

it's weird
i always remembered what he did
to me.
but the memories changed
over time
i used to think
he was just playing with me
but it didn't make sense
why did he take off his clothes
and mine?
why did he want to touch me
and make me touch him?
now, i know what he was doing
and why
and it makes me want to scream
but i can't
because what if i can't stop?

I wake up late, still tired from how badly I slept last night. I woke up a bunch of times in the middle of the night, and even though I was sleeping with Mom, I was still scared. I didn't know what I would think and dream next, and I just wanted to shut everything off, which was hard.

I'm not really feeling like going to the Center. Not today. But Mom has a meeting with one of her clients, the owner of a hair salon, to do some accounting work, and she doesn't want me staying home alone.

So I get dressed and go to the Center. We have Express Yo'self on Thursdays. Maybe that will help wake me up and take me outta my head.

I need to stop thinking.

At the Center, there are streamers and balloons around the cafeteria, so it has to be the birthday breakfast for all the senior citizens with August birthdays. Mrs. Prajapati comes out of the cafeteria with a smile on her face, and the music from inside floods out into the hallway.

I wave because she sees me and there's no way to walk by without saying hi. But really, I'm still embarrassed after crying like that in front of her, and after the night I had last night, I don't think I'll be able to talk to her without breaking down again. There's too much on my mind.

"I love that group," she says, still laughing. "So much fun."

"How many people had birthdays this month?"

"Seven. The oldest one is eighty-seven years old."

"Wow."

"We had the kindergarteners come in and sing 'Happy Birthday' to them, and they made paper flowers for everyone."

I smile. It reminds me of when I was little, when I came here for pre-K and kindergarten. We used to do things like that for the seniors, too.

"Were you able to learn the dance before the festival?" she asks me.

I shake my head. "I'll just be in the audience this time."

She tilts her head and gives me that *concerned* look. "Everything okay? You look tired."

I nod. "I'm alright."

She gives me a weak smile. "Good." Then we just look at each other and nobody says anything. So I say, "I'm taking Express Yo'self."

"Teddy has a nice, small group of writers. A dedicated group."

"Yeah, he makes me wanna get better."

"Well, go on then. And you know I'm here if you need to talk, right?"

I force myself to smile and nod. "Thanks."

I hurry away from her, down the hall, even though I'm way too early for the class. I just don't wanna risk crying again.

It's not until I'm around the corner that I breathe. I lift my head up and take some deep breaths. All I have to do is stop thinking.

Of course nobody is in the classroom yet. So I take the same seat I was in on Monday and take out my notebook. I flip through and realize Nicole was right. Everything I write *is* sad.

"You're early." It's Bree, the girl with the light blue hair, and she's standing right over me.

I close my notebook fast. "Oh, I didn't hear you."

"I'm like a cat," she says, laughing. "I sneak up on you!" She sits down next to me. "Is that whole book filled with poems?"

"Um, yeah, kinda. They're not really poems. Just like, thoughts, that—"

She holds her hand up to stop me from talking. "We have a rule around here. We never put our writing down. The world is hard enough for writers. We don't need to beat ourselves up, too."

I smile. I like that.

While we wait for the other kids to get there, me and Bree talk about all kinds of things. She goes to the achievement high school where Lana teaches, so she tells me all about it. "It's hard but good," she says. "They do give you homework for days, though!"

Oscar comes in next. He gives Bree a quick kiss on the lips, then sits across from us.

Bree says, "Oscar goes there, too. Caprice wants to know about our school."

"It's alright," he says. "Definitely the best school around here."

I tell them that my mom's best friend teaches math there, and when I tell them Lana's name, Oscar says, "I had her last year. She's cool, but she don't play!"

I laugh. "Yeah, that's her."

By the time the rest of the group gets going, I'm feeling a lot better. Relaxed. Like I'm actually part of this class.

Today, Teddy has the class do a warm-up exercise where we have to write a haiku beginning with the words "this is me." It takes me a while to write mine, probably because it's completely *not* me. But it doesn't embarrass me when Teddy asks us to read ours out loud.

this is me, trying

to have all my fun, one week

before school begins

"Why did you have to remind us about school?" the other boy, Mike, jokes, shaking his head at me. "I'm trying to stay in denial about it."

"Sorry," I tell him, laughing.

After everybody reads their haiku, Teddy talks to us about compression in poetry, how to say a lot with just a few words, just like in a haiku. And we practice and practice. I write a new haiku, a true one, but I keep it to myself.

> this is me, afraid
>
> of falling asleep, getting
>
> stuck in a nightmare

After we're done, Teddy says, "Y'all, we got two days before the festival. I know you have your poems ready, but I need you to practice. We need to blow these people's heads off, okay?"

"We're ready," Oscar says. "Don't worry."

Bree nods. "We got this, Teddy."

Then everybody turns to me like it's the first time they realize I have no poem for the festival. I never even said I would read anything.

"Caprice," Teddy says, "you're going to participate, right? We want to show everybody what Express Yo'self is about. Maybe get some more kids to join."

I can feel everyone staring at me. "But I don't have anything."

"That's a lie," Bree says. "I'm sorry, Caprice, but you know you have a notebook full of poems."

I open my mouth to defend myself. "But they're all sad and . . . I'm not as good as you guys."

"Read something," the girl from the basketball team says. "C'mon. You know we don't judge."

Now I'm on the spot. Everyone is looking at me, waiting. I feel my face get hot, but there's nothing I can do. I can't get out of this. So I pull out my notebook and flip through for something that's not too personal. Or embarrassing.

And I read them "memories, part one."

When I'm done, there's about three seconds of silence and then Oscar says, "Dude. You gotta read that. We need you."

I try to hide my smile. "No, you don't."

"Yeah, we do," Bree says. "You got that deep vibe. The rest of us are writing about dumb stuff."

"Hey!" Mike says, like he's offended. "*I'm* writing about my broken heart." He forces himself to make the most pitiful face possible.

Oscar throws his hands up. "Yeah, but you compare your broken heart to soggy Apple Jacks, man."

"I'm just saying they're both sad. It's called a metaphor!"

Next thing I know, we're all laughing.

"I'll think about it" is all I say.

I walk out of the classroom next to Bree. "So, is there a part two?" she asks me.

"Huh?" I have no idea what she's talking about.

She smiles. "Your poem."

"Oh, no. I don't know why I gave it that title. I should have—"

She puts her finger to her lips. "Remember, don't put yourself down. You gave it the title you wanted. If you want to change it later, you can. Or . . ."

"Or I can write a part two," I finish.

Oscar catches up to us, and he grabs Bree's hand. I have to admit, having a boyfriend is kinda cute. "We have to get to work," Bree tells me.

I wave to them and watch them walk off together.

As I pass the dance room, I slow down to peek inside. There's so much movement, and it all looks so good, so lively and fun, that it takes me a few minutes to realize Nicole isn't there dancing with them. Is she sick? I pull out my phone and text her.

u here?

She texts back right away.

gym

Why is she in the gym instead of dance? Even as I'm asking myself the question, I already know the answer. *Anthony.*

I head down the hall to the gym, where the boys from the baseball team are running laps. I see Rafa, too, but I don't know if he sees me. Nicole is standing by the table with a clear water jug. Two boys are standing next to her, and I watch as she fills up cups of water and hands it to them. When they go back to their workout, I walk up to her and ask, "So you were serious about becoming a ball girl?"

"No, I'm just helping out for a little while." She's actually smiling.

"Boys can get their own water, you know. Anyway, aren't you supposed to be in dance?"

"I told Abeni I had a headache and needed to rest."

She's not resting though. She's missing dance so she can look at Anthony. But I'm not gonna be the one to say any of that to her. Oh well. There's nothing for me to do until lunch, and I'm not gonna serve water with Nicole.

So I go over to the bleachers, sit down, and pull out my notebook.

when i was little

mom said
nobody has the right
to touch me
mom said
even people we know,
people we love
mom said
if it happens
i should tell her
mom said
she would believe me
no matter who it was

i knew
i should stay quiet,
never tell a soul
i knew
mom would get angry
or become really sad
i knew
it was her brother
and she loved him
i knew
when i told her
she would believe me

"What's wrong?"

Nicole slides next to me on the bleacher. She looks at my note-book, not like she's being nosy, but like she's worried.

But there's no way she can read this poem. I can't deal with the questions.

I close my notebook and say, "I'm still working on it" even though it's finished. "It's too . . ."

"Sad?" She's looking at my face now. "Are you crying?" Her face looks as sad as mine probably does.

I blink and realize tears *are* in my eyes. "No, not really. I was just thinking about something."

Remembering.

"Something you can't tell me about, right?"

A whistle blows and the baseball coach yells, "That's it for today, guys. Same time tomorrow."

The boys get up from the floor slowly, exhausted and in pain, and that's when I realize, I don't even remember when they got down there. Last I saw, they were running laps.

Nicole jumps up and goes back to the cooler, and she hands out cups of water to the boys as they come up to her. Rafa gets his water, and that's when he notices me. He smiles and waves, and I do the same. But I'm hoping he won't come over because I'm not sure I can pretend to be comfortable around him, not right now. Luckily, he starts talking to another guy, and the two of them walk out together.

Anthony waits to be last, and after Nicole gives him his water, the two of them talk and laugh together. I sit there and try to shake off the poem I was writing. I can't let myself sink into poems like that. Not here at the Center.

Next thing I know, Anthony is giving Nicole a quick kiss on the lips, and they're waving goodbye to each other. She watches as he gets his backpack and walks across the gym, and when he gets to the doors, just like I knew he would, he turns around and the two of them wave to each other again.

When Nicole comes back over to me, I ask her, "Where's Anthony going? He can't stay?"

"No, he has to get back to the pizzeria for the lunch crowd. His uncle keeps him busy."

"That's what you get for dating a working man!" We laugh, and I can feel the heaviness inside my chest lighten up, just a little.

We walk outta the gym, down the hall toward the bathroom where the other girls are probably already fixing themselves up before lunch.

"Okay," I say before we get there. "Tell me the truth. Why did you ditch dance? The festival is Saturday. Are you *that* good that you don't need to rehearse anymore?" I try to keep my voice light, like I'm kinda teasing her, but I'm serious.

"Don't worry about it. I only missed, like, the last twenty minutes or something. I already know the dance." We get near the bathroom and Nicole puts her arm around my shoulders and her face gets serious. "I know you think I only care about Anthony and dancing and all of that, but that's not true. You can talk to me."

I nod and look down. Nicole doesn't understand. It's not as easy as she thinks. Talking makes me feel. And feeling hurts.

We have archery again after lunch, but while we wait, I'm not in the mood to sit outside with the other girls. So I ask Nicole if she wants to walk to the store, but she's too busy styling Ayla's braids.

"I'll go with you," Jarrett says, coming up behind me. "Sorry. I wasn't, like, listening to you or anything, but I heard you and, um, my mom wants me to get her something from the store, so . . ."

"Stop doing that, Jarrett! Come on."

We head across the parking lot, and I know without a doubt that every single kid out there is watching us, especially the girls.

Since he doesn't say anything, I ask him if he has any new babies. Jarrett's mom is a foster parent, so there are always babies in his house.

"Yeah, and she's only six weeks old. And so chubby."

"I love when they're chubby!"

My hand accidentally brushes Jarrett's, but he doesn't react, so I'm not sure if he felt it.

"That's what I need from the store," Jarrett says. "Formula. But soy formula because she can't drink the other kind."

"You probably know everything about babies, right?"

"Kinda."

"I used to want a sister or brother when I was younger," I tell him. "But now, I'm kinda glad it's just me."

There's a car parked behind the barbershop that looks kinda like that car the nasty guy was fixing the other day. I'm not sure if it's the same though. Maybe. I walk closer to Jarrett just in case.

"I don't know if I'm supposed to ask," Jarrett begins, "but you girls, you gonna get your woman group or whatever?"

"Yeah, we start tomorrow. Thanks for your help, getting those sixth graders. I wish all boys were like you."

I tell Jarrett about the boys at the pool who were grading the girls. "Why do they have to be so sexist? Like, do they just see a girl's body or something?"

Jarrett shakes his head. "Sometimes boys, we think we gotta act like that, especially around girls. Like that makes us look cool. We talk about stuff like that in Man Group."

I never thought about it like that. I guess boys have a lot of pressure on them, too. But still. That's no excuse. "I'm still glad I yelled at those idiots!" I say. "They deserved it!"

Me and Jarrett turn the corner and walk to the bodega. I head straight for the Little Debbie rack. He gets three tall cans of formula and a bunch of loose Jolly Ranchers. "Zebra Cake?" he asks. "That's what you needed so bad?"

"I love these things! They're sweet and spongy and creamy!"

Jarrett stares at me while I talk, all the while trying to hide a smile, like he doesn't want me to know how much he likes me.

On the way outta the store, Jarrett's hand brushes against mine this time. I'm not sure if it's an accident, though, because when I look at him, he's taking deep breaths. I look away and wait a few seconds to see if he's finally gonna say what he wants to say.

We walk in silence, turning the corner and heading toward the parking lot.

Finally, Jarrett says, "I, um . . ." He does that breathing thing again. "I wanted to . . ." Breathe, breathe. "You were gone a long time, but before you went, I thought me and you, we were, you know . . ."

"Yeah, me too," I say. "We were, but . . ."

I stop talking because I don't know what I was gonna say. What *were* we before I left? I'm not sure.

I wish I could say going away helped me figure it all out, and I'm back home with answers. But the truth is, going away just helped me push all that stuff outta my mind so I didn't have to deal with it. And now we're in the exact same place we were in when I left.

Jarrett stops walking. This time he kinda sucks in a lot of air and then just blurts out, "I like you. A lot. And I'm not saying it because of your body and all of that, even though, yeah, I like that, too, but I'm saying it because I like *you*, and I just wanted to tell you that." He looks like he's gonna pass out.

It's hard to figure out how to respond to that, so all I do is smile. He's being so cute.

Before I can say anything, though, Jarrett looks down. "I know a smart girl like you might not like a guy like me, but . . ."

"I *do* like you," I say before I can stop myself. "I like you, and you're smart, too, so stop talking like that."

Jarrett looks at me, kinda frozen. "You like me? Like, for real?"

I nod, laughing.

We keep walking and, this time, when my hand touches his, it's not an accident. And then, Jarrett slowly takes my hand and we walk together like that, holding hands.

As we walk, I tell myself to relax. I can do this.

You're in control this time.

And no, I'm not sure what this means, but right now, I like it. It feels nice. Comfortable. And maybe that's good enough.

why me?

was it
my looks,
my loneliness,
my neediness?
was it me?
or was it him?

It's like the girls are *waiting* for me to get back. They're still hanging outside behind the Center, and they all stand up when we get close, like they can't wait to question me.

By then, me and Jarrett have stopped holding hands, and we're just talking about cartoons like that's all we were talking about the whole time. He even asks me if I wanna be a voice of one of his characters, and of course I'm, like, "Yeah!"

I don't get to say goodbye to Jarret because the girls circle around me. "What happened?" Nicole asks. "Dee-tails!"

Everyone's staring at me for the first time ever. And they're excited for me. It's strange but I actually feel kinda happy, like I'm part of their club or something.

I laugh. "Come on, guys. All we did was walk to the store and back. That's it!"

Ayla shakes her head. "I can see it in your eyes. Y'all kissed!"

"*What?*" I cover my mouth.

Gina and Yesenia are nodding, smiling.

"We didn't kiss!"

Ayla is still looking at me like she thinks I'm lying. "You surprised me just now, walking off with him. I didn't think you even looked at the boys around here."

Why would she say that?

Nicole adds, "Yeah, we thought you were only thinking about the Ainsley boys." She says *Ainsley* real fancy.

I roll my eyes. "Ainsley is all-girls," I mumble, but suddenly I'm boiling inside. "There *are* no boys."

Nicole shrugs. "Just saying. I didn't think you even noticed any of the guys from here. Jarrett's been drooling after you for, like, *years*!"

She laughs. Then they all laugh. And I just want this conversation to be over already. Now I know they've been talking about me behind my back, saying that I think I'm too good for the boys around here when that's not even true.

I was part of their club for about eight seconds.

• • • • • •

All through archery, me and Jarrett don't say anything to each other. We don't even look at each other. I don't need to give the girls anything else to gossip about me over, especially Nicole.

After archery, Mrs. Prajapati makes us take some kinda class where this teacher tries to get us ready for the new school year, which starts in a week here in Newark.

Of course, if I go back to Ainsley, I need to be back on Sunday. Three days from now.

All through the class, I'm still upset. Still thinking about what Nicole said. Still wondering what else she says about me when I'm not around.

The teacher gives out academic planners and new pens and stuff, and then we're technically done for the day. It's only 4:00. If I rush home, I can call Dr. Suzanne before she leaves her office. I can give her my decision.

But while we're leaving the classroom, Nicole whispers to me, "What's wrong?"

I shrug. If she doesn't know, I'm not telling her.

"Come." Nicole literally grabs my arm and drags me down the hall and around the corner toward our pre-K class.

"We can't," I say.

"It's okay. They're on a trip." We slip into the classroom, and Nicole closes the door behind us. I walk to the other side of the room and stare out the window for a little while.

"You're mad?" Nicole sounds like she's surprised that I can get mad.

I shrug.

"Okay, you're mad. Why?"

I look around the room, everywhere except in her direction. Finally, I ask, "Why did you say that?"

"Say what?"

"That I only like boys at Ainsley, which isn't even a thing, and I'm too good to think about the boys around here. And how do you know what I'm thinking about?"

"I don't know. I just know that you're back here, but you're still there. Your head is definitely not here."

I cross my arms in front of me. "What if I have other things on my mind? You ever thought of that?"

Nicole's eyes get so wide. "What are you talking about? How many times did I ask you what was going on? And now you're turning on *me*?"

I look away. "Whatever."

We're quiet. I look around the classroom. Since we were here on Saturday, there's new artwork. Little graduation caps with the kids' names on them. And on top of the caps there's a huge banner that reads, *Good Luck in Kindergarten!*

It's hard not to smile. I kinda remember my pre-K graduation. I think.

Nicole sits on the teacher's desk. "What's on your mind, then? Tell me."

"Everything," I whisper.

"Is it about Jarrett?"

"No, I mean, kinda. It's everything all mixed together." And again, I feel tears start to slide down my face. "There's something wrong with me."

Her voice is quiet, too, when she says, "Talk to me."

I don't know where to start, so I start at Ainsley, about the party we had on Friday night. I tell Nicole about how excited everybody was, not just for the party but for the Kentworth boys who were gonna be there.

"This girl in the dorm—she's from the Philippines, and she's an amazing dancer—she was giving everyone dance lessons in her room. It was so much fun."

That part was fun.

"At the party, there was a boy."

Nicole sits up a little straighter. "I knew there was a boy! You can't have a party without *boys*!" She tries to laugh a little bit, but it's not working.

"The party. It was fun. Really fun. The music was good, and everybody was dancing."

Just thinking about it brings me back to the party. I'm here talking to Nicole, but I'm gone. My mind is back there. So I tell her. "At first, the girls were just dancing together, basically ignoring the boys. But then the boys got brave and came over and asked some girls to dance. Isaiah came up to me because we already knew each other.

"It was cute the way he asked me to dance. He looked shy. Everybody else was dancing, and I think I just got tired of being so different all the time. So I said okay, and we danced. It was a fast song, so it was kinda fun. Before I knew it, we were laughing and talking."

"That sounds good. So far."

"It was. So when Isaiah asked me if I wanted to go down to the lake where a lot of other kids were going, I said okay. Sure. My friends Deja and Terra were gonna be there, too, and it was a real pretty night. My last night there."

I glance over to Nicole, and she's still looking at me. Paying attention.

So I keep talking. "On the way down to the lake, Isaiah put his hand on my back to make sure I didn't trip on a branch. It wasn't *that* dark outside, but it was getting hard to see. I didn't think anything of it. I just thought he was being a gentleman, like in the old movies I watch with Mom. We walked a little more, and through the trees I could see the lake and some of the kids who were hanging out around it. I started to relax. And that was when it happened. Isaiah put his hand on my shoulder, and he leaned closer to me and put his mouth on mine so fast I couldn't really figure out what was going on for a few seconds."

Nicole's eyes get wide. "What did you do?"

"It was like I was in shock," I tell her. "I couldn't move. I never got kissed before, and it wasn't only his lips on me. His hands were on my back. And the way he was breathing. I was alone in the woods with this boy I didn't really know, and I just got, I don't know, scared."

I was frozen.

"He shouldn't have done that," Nicole says. "You're not supposed to kiss someone if they don't want it."

"I know, but . . ." I shake my head. "I panicked. I felt . . ."

I felt trapped.

If I keep talking I'm gonna say too much, and then I'm gonna fall apart again. So I stop talking and try to suck my feelings back inside.

Finally, Nicole says, "Don't worry. Forget about it. You never have to see that guy again." She's saying the right things to make me feel better. But it doesn't work.

I have to tell her. I wanted to wait until I made a decision, but I can't keep this from her any longer.

I swallow hard and say, "There's more. It's not really . . . It's not, like, for sure or anything. It's just that, the head of the school, Dr. Suzanne, um, she offered me a scholarship to go back for eighth grade."

Nicole looks stunned. "But what about—"

"*And* high school."

The look on Nicole's face is like frustration and anger and sadness all rolled into one. And the sigh she lets out feels like one she's been holding in for a long time. She wanted to know what I was keeping to myself, and now she knows.

I can't help but feel like I've knocked the wind out of her. I've crushed her.

"I'm sorry," I whisper. "I wanted to tell you, but—"

"Forget it," she says, holding her hand up like she's trying to stop me from talking.

But I still have to make her understand. "I haven't even decided yet. It's a big decision. It could change my whole—"

"You're leaving," Nicole interrupts me. "You know you're going and so do I. So just stop."

She jumps off the desk and walks right outta the room without even saying anything else.

She's done with me.

I don't get home till it's too late to call Dr. Suzanne. I probably could have called her from the Center and caught her before she left work, but I still need to figure out what to say to her.

I need more time.

While Mom works, I go to my room and lie down before dinner. I feel like so much happened today. Yeah, I keep thinking about Jarrett, but it's Nicole's face I can't forget. Why didn't I tell her right away that I might be leaving?

There's no way to undo what I did to her. Except stay here.

At dinner, Mom says, "You have to come home early tomorrow."

"I know."

"It's our last chance to call Dr. Suzanne."

"I know."

But I don't know when my phone call to Dr. Suzanne became something *we* need to do. I thought it was *my* decision, my call. Anyway, she knows I know I have to call. Why does she keep reminding me?

It's like she's pushing me.

So I just ask her. "Mom, do you wanna go back to Detroit? I mean, are you only staying here because of me?"

"What? Why . . . ?" Mom stares at me and shakes her head. "Why would you think something like that? This is where I live. And of course I'm here because of you."

I look down. "I mean, if I go back to Ainsley, would that, you know, be easier for you and Dad? And better for the business? Because I don't wanna be the reason the business—"

"Caprice, there's no one and nothing more important than you.

Even the business. And yeah, I miss your father, but we've been apart a lot this year."

"I know. That's what I'm saying. I want you and him to be the way you were before."

Mom comes around the table and puts her arms around me. "Don't worry about any of that. If you want to go back to Ainsley, I will support you. And if you want to stay here, I will love spending more time with you."

Mom is acting like she doesn't know what I'm asking her. So I try again. "But would it be easier if I just went back?"

Mom shakes her head. "It would be easier for the business. But it wouldn't be easier on *me*. I would miss you."

I let Mom hug me, but I still don't know what I'm gonna do. My mind is too all over the place.

So me and Mom eat dinner, and just as we're about to start washing dishes, Terra texts me. It's a picture of her and her mom in front of the hugest, most beautiful mountains. She writes:

> hiked bright angel trail! leaving tomorrow. mum has to get to dc for a state dinner at the white house sat night! fancy!!

I text back:

> wow. send pictures when she's dressed up!

> you got it!

I miss her.

"Do you want to sleep with me again?" Mom asks me when the kitchen is clean. "We can watch a movie or—"

"No, I'm okay."

"Aw." She kisses me on the forehead. "Let's do it before you leave though."

I nod. It's just that I need to be alone tonight.

In my room, I take out my notebook, but not to write a poem this time. Just to think on paper.

On top of the page I write AINSLEY in big letters. Then I make two columns and start filling them in:

PROS	CONS
Something new and challenging.	Will miss Mom & Dad.
School is amazing.	Will miss my school & the Center.
Will let Mom and Dad be together!!!!!!	I might get homesick.
Will help our business.	Will really really really miss Nicole.
I will be safe.	I think I'm starting to like Jarrett.

I don't know if I was looking for a winner, but it's a 5–5 tie. And I still don't know what to do.

two uncle raymonds

when i was little
i thought
there were two of them.
the one who played with dinosaurs and barbies
and watched disney movies with me
and the one who never had time for any of that
who only wanted to do one thing
over and over.
even now
it's hard to believe
they were both the same person.

Me and Mom go shopping all morning, making sure I have all the clothes and underwear and girl stuff I need to get through the first couple of months at Ainsley. I don't even get to the Center until lunchtime, and as soon as I walk into the cafeteria, I know something's up. Something's changed.

I don't know if Nicole wants me to sit next to her, but that's the only seat that's empty. As soon as I sit, Ayla eyes me up and down and says, "We thought you were gone already. Don't let us hold you up."

I can't believe this.

I turn to Nicole. "You *told* them?"

She doesn't really look at me. "Was it a secret? Don't you think people would notice if you're not here anymore?"

I've been at the Center for five minutes and I'm already steaming. But I'm not letting them get to me.

So I tell Ayla, "I haven't made a decision yet. I wish I could be in two places."

"But you can't be," she says.

"Yeah," Nicole says. "Pick who you wanna be with."

Sounds so easy when she says it. Wish it was that easy in real life.

⬩—•—•—•—⬩

After lunch, the girls have dress rehearsal for the festival tomorrow. Nicole still hasn't really said a word to me. She just walks away, toward the dance room, leaving me standing in the hall alone.

"Good. You're here." It's Jarrett. He and Ennis are carrying microphones and a bunch of cables and stuff. "You ready to record your voice?"

I forgot all about that, but I'm glad I have somewhere to go, something to do. Ennis walks ahead of us down the hall, and me and Jarrett look at each other and smile. I wait for him to say something about Ainsley, ask me if it's true I'm leaving, but he doesn't.

Nicole probably didn't have time to tell my secret to *everybody* yet.

We follow Ennis into the computer room, and after they set everything up, Jarrett hands me the script. "You play Rax."

"What kind of person is she?" I ask.

"Well, she's not a person exactly," Ennis says. "She's a very nice sewer rat who helps—"

"A sewer rat? What?" My voice comes out louder than I thought. "I thought I was gonna be a sweet little bunny rabbit or something!"

Jarrett laughs. "Rax is really cute, um, you know . . . for a sewer rat."

Now Ennis joins him and they're both laughing. I mutter under my breath, "I'm a cute sewer rat."

Now all three of us are laughing. It takes us a while to get serious. But when Jarrett hands me a pair of huge headphones that fit over my whole ears, I feel professional right away.

Rax has only five lines, so she's not the star, but the whole cartoon is only two minutes and forty seconds, so I'm happy to have a part. And when Ennis shows me Rax on the computer, she *is* kinda cute. And kinda wet and dirty.

When I'm done, Jarrett's brother Kevon shows up in the computer room to record his part. While Ennis puts the headphones on him and gives him the script, me and Jarrett move away from them, all the way to the other side of the room.

We sit together, close, and whisper to each other whenever

Ennis and Kevon stop recording. "I was gonna text you last night," Jarrett says, "but I didn't want you to think I was a stalker."

"That makes no sense!"

"Okay, I'll text you tonight," he says.

I smile. "Good."

Ennis puts his hand up so we can stop talking, and we sit there quietly, waiting until we can talk again.

I can't stop thinking about Nicole and how she told everybody my business. She keeps saying I can tell her anything, but it's hard to trust her all of a sudden.

I have to tell Jarrett, too, especially now that everybody else knows. But this isn't the right time. We need to be alone.

"Do you have to go straight home today?" I ask him, keeping my voice extra low so Ennis and Kevon won't hear us.

"No, not really. Why?" He looks kinda excited.

"Can you walk me home?"

"Yeah, definitely."

"Good. I'll see you later." I wave goodbye and leave the computer room.

I don't really feel like spending more time with Nicole and the girls who talk about me behind my back, but it's time for Woman Group.

I'm the first one to get to Woman Group, which kinda makes sense, since I'm the one who started this whole thing. For some reason, I'm feeling nervous. Like, is everyone who signed up gonna show up? Are all these girls gonna get along? Is this even gonna work?

Oh well, it's too late now.

The seats are arranged in a circle, so I sit near the window, so I can see everyone as they come in. And since I have time, I try to finish *Breath, Eyes, Memory*. Lana is coming over tonight to talk about the end, and I need to be ready.

I'm just finishing the book when Nicole shows up. She's early, too, but just a little. She hardly even looks at me. She just takes a seat on the other side of the circle, as far away from me as she can get. Then she sighs real loud, like three or four times.

Finally, I say, "What?"

She looks at me like she's now noticing me. "Nothing."

We're quiet for a few seconds.

Then she says, "It's just that, you're the one that wanted this group. This Woman Group. And now, we finally have it, and what are you doing? You're leaving. Tell me that makes sense."

"It's not that simple," I say. "You expect me to turn down an opportunity like this?"

"So that's it? You're really going?"

"I don't know. I still have to call the head of school and tell her I accept."

Nicole folds her arms in front of her. "What are you waiting for?"

"I don't know. Maybe something that's gonna change my mind."

"Wow." She actually looks at me like I hurt her. "So your best friend doesn't make you wanna stay? Fine." She gives a shrug, and she looks down and digs through her backpack.

I watch her while I try to figure out what to say. "That's not what I meant, Nicole. You know that." I take a deep breath and try to calm myself down. It's like she's attacking me for no reason. "I'm just saying this scholarship is a big deal. And yeah, I'm gonna miss you, but I can't be in two places at the same time."

"So you picked a *school* over me. And what, you're gonna miss my party? Just like that? And you couldn't tell me before now? I had everything planned out, and now—"

"God!" I say, a little too loud. "It's not all about you! Why is everything about you?"

Me and her glare at each other, but before she can say anything back, a woman walks into our classroom. And right away I know. Our brand-new Woman Group leader just caught us in the middle of a girl fight.

Great.

The woman looks older than a college student, but still kinda young. She's wearing a long, colorful summer dress and sandals, and her hair is natural, pulled high on top of her head in a wild puff. She looks cool, down-to-earth. Something about her makes me feel comfortable, like she's gonna be someone we can open up to.

The first thing she does is point to the book that's still in my hand and say, "That book is so powerful, isn't it?"

I nod and say, "Every sentence is like reading poetry."

"Do you write poetry?"

I nod again. "Kinda." Then I remember what Bree always says about not putting down my writing, so I add, "I write all the time."

I wait for Nicole to say something about my poems, about how sad and depressing they are, but she doesn't say anything. She's still just staring at me.

"Keep doing it," the woman says. "We need more poets in the world."

• • • • •

The first Woman Group is everything I want it to be. Our group leader is named Zoe Branch, and she's a graduate student at Rutgers. She tells us she's studying women's studies, so this kinda group is something she's really excited about.

Zoe starts the group by asking us, "What are some of the misconceptions people have about girls?"

Gina is the first to answer. "That we're weak," she says.

Zoe writes that on the whiteboard. *Girls are weak.*

"That we're shallow," Yesenia says. "That all we care about is what we look like and our clothes and stuff."

Zoe writes *Girls are shallow* on the board.

Then everybody starts calling out misconceptions, so many, so fast.

"That we're not good at math and science and engineering and all that stuff."

"That we're all mean to each other."

"That our sports aren't as fun and important as boys' sports."

I think about the way everybody couldn't believe I spent a whole summer at an all-girls school and say, "That we need boys around to have fun, like it's not good enough when it's just us."

One of the sixth graders says, "Everyone thinks all girls are boy crazy."

Gina shakes her head and says, "I'm not."

"Me neither," Yesenia says, giggling. "I'm *girl* crazy!"

Zoe writes on the board: *Girls only care about boyfriends or girlfriends.*

Now that it's written on the board, it's easy to see how untrue it is. I mean, we care about a lot more than that. Like Yesenia. She likes girls *and* art. Even Nicole and Ayla like dance and drama and all kinds of things besides boys.

"A lot of people think our opinions don't matter," Nicole says.

Zoe writes *Girls have no opinions.*

When we all finish answering the question, the whole white-board is filled, and it's really crazy. And sad. If someone walked into this classroom, all they would see is a board that says girls are dumb, girls are too emotional, girls need protection, and all kinds of stuff like that. And we probably could have kept going if we had more time.

"That's depressing," Ayla says, and we all agree.

And we keep talking about it and why we think people think this way about women. Then Zoe erases the board and we fill it with the truth about women, how strong and smart and caring and funny and friendly and awesome we really are.

Zoe doesn't erase those words. She tells us, "This is the kind of thing we're going to talk about here every week. We're going to discuss our feelings and our experiences, and we're going to build each other up and support one another because the world out there is hard for girls. We have to deal with *a lot*, and we need our sisters to lean on. We need to know we have each other's backs."

We all look at one another. I wonder if I'll *ever* feel that way about these girls. Hopefully.

Zoe makes us stand up and hold hands. She even joins us in our circle. "This is a safe space for women to talk," she tells us. "Everyone, repeat after me: What we say here will be kept private. What we say here will be respected. What we say here will be believed."

We all repeat the three sentences all together. Then we say it again and again.

Then Zoe says, "The same goes for outside of this classroom, too. The women in this group honor each other, no matter where we are." She lets this sink in for a little while, and I try not to look at Nicole. She shouldn't have told everyone my business, but tomorrow is our last sleepover before I leave. Maybe we can start over again.

For the rest of Woman Group, Zoe talks to us about feminism, and we discuss what it means to us. I never really thought about it before. Maybe I thought I was too young or something. But I'm all about equality for women. Who wouldn't be?

After we're done, Zoe tells us she'll see us next week. Everyone waves goodbye, and I can't help but feel sad. Woman Group was just what I needed. Too bad it will be my first and last.

Jarrett is waiting for me when we come outta the classroom. I'm feeling kinda tingly from the class, like it was just the start of something I won't have again. Even if Ainsley has a group like this, it won't have Zoe.

I say goodbye to the sixth-grade girls and, before I can go over to where Jarrett is standing, Nicole comes up to me. I'm thinking she's going to say something about our argument, but no. She says, "I'm canceling our sleepover tomorrow.

Anthony and I are gonna hang out after the festival. So . . ."

"You're skipping our sleepover?" I can't believe what she's saying. "Just because of a dumb argument?"

"Sorry." Nicole shrugs. "But remember, you left first. You're the one that broke the chain."

On the way home, Jarrett and I talk about his little foster sister, archery class, back-to-school shopping. What I don't talk about is what just happened with Nicole and how I'm feeling about it, because I'm not about to let what she did get to me. I'm not gonna care that she ditched our sleepover for Anthony. She can do whatever she wants.

"Oh, yeah," Jarrett says. He unzips his backpack and pulls out a Zebra Cake. "I got this for you."

I smile so big. "You didn't have to do that!"

"I went to the store while I was waiting for you." He unwraps a Jolly Rancher and pops it in his mouth.

I take a bite of the Zebra Cake. "So good," I tell him. I almost say something about how I'm gonna miss these when I'm away, but I haven't told him about that yet. I know I have to, I *need* to, but it feels like I'm putting a stop to something right as it's getting started. It doesn't feel fair to either one of us.

We walk and talk, and because I'm with Jarrett I don't walk the long way like I've been doing. And suddenly I see it just a few doors down. My old house.

"You okay?" Jarrett asks me. "You kinda faded away, like in a movie."

I shake my head. "Sorry. It's just that, this is my house. My old house, I mean. And I . . . this is the first time I'm seeing it up close since . . ."

"Since you moved out?"

"Yeah." I stop walking and just look at it. It looks the same. Only now, near the driveway, there's a little kid's basketball hoop, the plastic kind that's painted yellow and red.

Some other kid lives there now.

I knew another family was living there, but I guess I just didn't wanna have to see it up close. In my face. Because now I know for a fact we'll never live here again.

"It's okay," I say, more to myself than Jarrett. "My family, we didn't need a whole house anymore. It's okay."

Jarrett grabs hold of my hand. "But that doesn't mean it's not hard, right?"

"Right."

We walk past the house quietly, and we don't start talking again until we're on the next block. I'm kinda happy I did that.

It was time to let that house go.

While we walk, Jarrett says, "Ever since you got back, it's like you're different. I'm not saying you're . . . You're still nice, but you're kinda sad."

True.

"I mean, I know it's not my business or anything, but—"

"It's okay, Jarrett. I'm just going through a lot of stuff right now. My grandmother is really sick, and I have to make a decision about something that's really important."

"Maybe I can help. I mean, if you want help."

We get near my house, so I slow down. I don't wanna get there too fast. That's when I tell him. "I got offered a scholarship to Ainsley. It's a great school, and I loved it there. But I love it here, too. So . . ."

"So you don't know what to do." Jarrett looks sad, but I don't know if he's sad that I have to make this decision, or sad I'm leaving.

"Yeah. I think I should go. It's too big an opportunity. It could change my life."

Jarrett looks down. "I'll miss you if you go."

"I'll miss you, too."

And that's when it happens. Jarrett picks his head up and looks directly in my eyes. "I'll miss you more," he says, and leans closer to me. I lean closer to him, too, and the next thing I know, our lips are pressed together.

And this kiss is so sweet, and not just because Jarrett's lips taste like green Jolly Rancher. It's sweet because I know he really likes me.

It's nothing like the way Isaiah kissed me that night, hard and long. This kiss is fast, just lips connecting. And when we pull away, Jarrett looks at me like he wants to be sure it's okay with me.

It is.

But instead of telling him that, I lean in and kiss him again. And even as I do it, I feel my body relax, because this is what I wanna do. I want this.

A minute later, I tell Jarrett I need to go. "I have to call the head of the school to tell her I'm gonna accept the offer."

Jarrett nods. "Are you gonna be there tomorrow, to see our cartoon at the festival?"

I smile. "Yeah, of course. Wouldn't miss it. And I'm reading a poem."

"Oh, okay. Good. I wanna hear it."

We don't kiss again. I just thank Jarrett for walking me home, and we wave goodbye. He heads back toward the Center and I walk the rest of the way home. I'm smiling. I can't help it.

I wish that was my first kiss.

At home, I actually think about telling Mom about the kiss. That's how excited I am. But then I decide to keep it to myself for a little while longer.

On the kitchen table, Mom has the Ainsley book open and she's writing lists and all kinda information on a notepad.

"What are you doing?" I ask her.

"Just thinking of all the questions I'm going to have for Dr. Suzanne. I was looking through the book. There are so many things this school can offer you, so many classes and clubs and trips, and so many things to try."

"Yeah," I say, and it kinda hits me. "But shouldn't everybody be able to do those things, not just a bunch of girls at a fancy boarding school?"

"It's not fair, Caprice. Nobody is saying it is. Those girls have a lot more opportunities than everyone else. But at least the school is trying to help kids like you get these experiences."

I sit down at the table and glance up at the clock on the stove. I have a half hour to make the biggest decision of my life.

Then I ask Mom quietly, "Why did you tell Dr. Suzanne I would accept the offer before you talked to me about it?"

"We said yes because your father and I knew how happy you were there." She reaches for her phone and taps a few things. Then she hands the phone to me. "Look."

It's our text messages from when I was at Ainsley. Selfies of me and Terra in our dorm room, me and Deja on our college trip, posing in front of an MIT sign, a picture Deja took of Terra trying to teach me how to dive. No matter what the picture was about, I look as happy as I've ever been.

I loved being there.

As I scroll through the texts, one of them makes me stop. It's just a picture Terra took of me and Deja working on our project in the library. We're sitting in front of a huge window with the sun setting behind us. It's a beautiful picture. Underneath I wrote:

> i wonder what it's like going to school here. a girl can dream!

"That's why we thought we could accept for you. You'd told us what you wanted."

She's right. If I'd been in Dr. Suzanne's office with them, I would have accepted in, like, two seconds. "Okay," I say. "But next time, can you just ask me first?"

"Deal." Mom sits at the table. Before I can even say anything else, her cell rings. "I have to get this."

She starts talking, and I know it's probably somebody from the hospital. She says something about kidney failure, and I know that's real bad. "Her son, my brother, he's on his way home from Germany," she tells whoever it is. "He's in the military, so I don't know what flight he'll be able to get."

Grandma only has one son. Uncle Raymond.

> he said
>
> touch it

I can't listen to Mom's conversation anymore.

> he said
>
> do it
>
> i'll show you how

I grab my cell from my backpack and practically run down

the hall to my room. I have to catch Dr. Suzanne before it's too late.

> he said
>
> that's it
>
> just like that

My heart is racing as I find her number in my phone and wait for her to answer.

> he said
>
> don't say anything
>
> to anyone
>
> not anyone

And then finally, I hear, "This is Dr. Suzanne."

I feel a wave of nervousness flutter across my stomach. "Hi, Dr. Suzanne. This is Caprice. Caprice Barnes." Like there's another Caprice at the school.

"Caprice." Her friendly voice instantly relaxes me. "I've been expecting your call. You kept me in suspense."

"I'm sorry. It's just that it's a big decision."

"I can only imagine."

This is it. I need to tell her what I decided. "I'd love to come back to Ainsley. Being there changed my life, and I'm really excited to become a student there because I know I'll be challenged."

"That you will be," Dr. Suzanne says. "This is wonderful, Caprice. We're looking forward to having you."

"Thank you so much."

I talk to Dr. Suzanne for another minute or two, and then I thank her again before we hang up. I sit there on my bed for a few minutes actually feeling kinda relieved. I did it. I'm going back to Ainsley.

I'm leaving.

Back in the kitchen, Mom is still on the phone, still talking about Grandma. I can tell she's really worried. *Grandma is getting worse.* The weird thing is they're talking about someone I remember but don't really know. She's a grandmother who is basically a stranger to me.

When Mom finally hangs up, there are tears in her eyes. I was gonna tell her I called Dr. Suzanne, but instead, I ask her if Grandma is gonna be alright.

She gives a half shrug. "We don't know. Nobody knows."

Seeing Mom this sad makes me begin to cry, too. Most of this is my fault. I know that. But at the same time it feels like a door is closing that I might never be able to open again. "I don't know her," I say through my tears. "And now, what if I never—?"

"All of this was Grandma's choice, baby," Mom says quietly. "We didn't just pick up one day and decide to move away. We were *asked to leave* Grandma's house. With nowhere to go, mind you. Thank God Lana invited us to move to Newark. She let us stay with her for *months* until we could find a place we could afford. It was a rough time."

I don't say anything.

"I know you probably don't remember what happened, but somehow you got out of the house by yourself. You got lost. The police got involved. The lead story on the news was the search for the missing Baltimore girl. It was all really scary."

I swallow hard.

Mom grabs my hand in both of hers. "After all of that chaos, I don't know, I think Grandma panicked or something. She threw us out of her house. It was wrong, not something I'll ever get over. I mean, how do you throw out a mother with a little child in the middle of the night? In the middle of winter?"

I remember all of that.

Mom wipes her tears. "And now I'm supposed to forget all of it? I'm supposed to go down there to Baltimore and take care of her? How am I supposed to do that?"

I don't know. But I'm getting scared. Scared something's gonna happen with Grandma, and I'll never get to know her. Scared Mom will change her mind and decide she *does* need to go back to Baltimore. Scared I won't be able to get away before we have to go back.

Scared I might break.

pain

surrounds me
suffocates me
fills my body chokes my heart
breaks me in half crushes what's left

what's left?

• • • •

Later, Lana comes over and brings Mexican food with her so we can celebrate. I don't know why, but that's when everything feels really real. I'm leaving. Lana hugs me a million times, saying things like, "I'm so happy for you." And then five minutes later, "I don't want to let you go."

Talk about mixed messages!

But I get it. I'm having all those feelings, too. In two days, I'll be back at Ainsley, but am I even ready? And what's it gonna be like when Mom and Dad leave me there this time, not for seven weeks, but for months? I probably won't be able to come home until Thanksgiving.

Just thinking about it makes me kinda shaky. Good thing Mom and Lana are there to keep me from thinking about it too much.

Before we eat, I call Dad and tell him I made my decision, but he tells me he already knew what I was gonna do. "No way would a daughter of mine turn down an opportunity like that," he says. And, of course, he tells me how proud he is and all that, and how he'll be home early Sunday to drive me back to Ainsley. "Love you," he says.

"Love you, too." I miss him.

• • • •

A little later, after we've torn through most of the tacos, and I'm kneeling on the floor beside the table in the living room finishing my nachos and salsa, I decide the time is right. "Mom, Lana," I say. "Guess what?" I start giggling too much to wait for them to guess. "Jarrett and I kissed today."

Mom's mouth flies open at the same time Lana joins me on the floor. "Tell me everything!"

It's kinda embarrassing, but I tell them what I can remember about the kiss, how nervous Jarrett was, the way his lips tasted, and how I'm the one who kissed him the second time.

"I. Am. Stunned," Mom says, with a half smile on her face. "My little baby is running around kissing boys on the street!"

"Taught her everything I know," Lana says.

Mom shakes her head. "Good thing I'm shipping her off to an all-girls school."

We all laugh.

Later, after me and Lana discuss the end of *Breath, Eyes, Memory*, and after Mom and Lana help me organize and start packing my clothes and stuff, I stay in my room texting while Mom and Lana have a glass of wine in the living room. I text Deja and Terra to let them know it's official. I'm coming back. It's fun, seeing how happy they are. I can't wait to see them again.

And I can't wait to get back there, to get that second chance I've been wanting ever since the party. A do-over. I'll be stronger this time. I'll hold on tighter.

That night, after I ran away from Isaiah, I remember feeling kinda sick, queasy, in the pit of my stomach. I didn't wanna deal with those feelings. Couldn't. I just wanted to push everything down and not think about it.

I was crying, but why? It was just a kiss. He didn't hurt me. He liked me.

But still, at the lake, I searched for Terra and found her sitting with another girl from the swim team. I waved to get her attention and she came over to me. "I need to get outta here" is all I said. "Now."

About a minute later, just barely away from all the other kids, I became a mess.

I could still feel his hands on me. I could still feel his lips on mine. I was shaking and shaking, and I knew in my head that what I was feeling was too much for what happened. It felt like my reaction was coming from somewhere else inside me, too far down for me to reach, and my reaction scared me.

Terra brought me back to our room, and she wiped my face and listened to me tell her how sorry I was for whatever was happening to me. I was sorry for dragging her into this.

But she kept telling me it was okay and she got me to lie down. She left the room for a few minutes, and by the time she got back, I had stopped crying. I was more embarrassed than scared. That panicky feeling came from nowhere.

Terra sat on my bed next to me and she told me everything was gonna be alright. I wanted to believe her.

And I wanted to explain what happened. Only I didn't know. A boy who I'd danced with all night kissed me. I knew he should have asked me first, but maybe he thought I liked him, too. He just didn't know how messed up I was.

After a while, me and Terra talked about other things. She even tried to make me laugh. My chest was still heavy with tears, but I decided to keep them there. Even as we changed outta our party clothes and got ready for bed, I was still feeling kinda weak and exhausted from crying so much.

Luckily, Terra took care of me that night. Because I couldn't take care of myself.

. . . . .

The Center is crazy, even more than usual. Everybody is rushing around, scrambling to get ready for the Cultural Festival in the afternoon.

"C'mon, people," Andre, one of the group leaders, yells from the hall. "The first bus is getting ready to leave. If you need to set up your project, you need to leave now."

From around the corner, some kids come out of the art room with huge poster boards and some kinda bird sculpture that's made out of wire and leaves that looks like it's gonna fall apart before it gets to the bus.

Another bunch of kids come running outta the music room carrying their clarinets and flutes in cases. They're followed by three teenage boys with their guitars and keyboards strapped to their backs. They created their own indie band called Dog Robot and played at the block party in July. I can't wait to hear them today.

As I walk down the hall, I pass other kids running for the bus, all of them either carrying some kinda project or wearing a costume. It feels weird that all I'm doing is reading a poem. Most of the time I'm in the dance. And I usually end up helping out in the children's tent, too. Last year, I was one of the face painters, which was really fun. Maybe I'll do something like that again this year.

But I'm gonna have to catch the next bus because I'm not ready to go over there yet.

On my way down the hall, I pass by the dance room, and through the little window on the door, I can see they're having another rehearsal. Abeni is in front of the room saying something, but I can't hear her over the loud African music. The girls are dancing much better than the last time I saw them, and those beautiful blue dresses are gonna look so nice on the stage. Everyone is gonna love them.

I'm still peeking into the window when Nicole spins around, arms high in the air, and before I can duck out of the way, her eyes catch mine. I wish I could talk to her, now that she's at least giving me a little attention. There's so much I wanna ask her, like why she really ditched our sleepover. Is she really choosing Anthony over me?

And I want her to know it's official. I'm going back to Ainsley tomorrow. Tonight would have been our last sleepover for a long time.

But how can I tell her? And when?

It doesn't matter, though, because one second after she sees me, she looks away, and she's back to her dance without missing a step. I wait another few moments, but she never looks my way again.

And that's it.

But I'm okay. For now. I'm not gonna think about it. I can't. I have something else to do, and I wanna be alone anyway.

The computer room is empty, just like I knew it would be. I have time to do my research here, where Mom won't see what I'm doing. I don't wanna hear her questions, wondering what I'm looking for and why. I just wanna know the truth and keep it to myself.

The first thing I do is google my name and scroll through some mentions of me from school when I won an award or something. It doesn't take long until I see her.

The little girl I used to be.

It's hard to see myself in her. She looks like me, only with a rounder face and chubbier cheeks. She even has her braids pulled back in a ponytail, the same way I wear my locs now. But something about her is so different. It's my eyes. They're so sad. Afraid.

It's an old newspaper article from eight years ago. The headline reads, *Missing West Baltimore Girl Found Safe.*

The article talks about how a woman who was doing her laundry at the 24-Hour Wash & Fold on Washington Boulevard found the little girl, who had been missing since around 10:30 p.m. She was only wearing a nightgown and no coat or shoes.

I still remember the cold. I remember the chaos.

The article says the police responded to the scene. The child seemed to be in shock and unable to speak, so she was taken to the hospital.

I could have answered their questions. I just didn't wanna go home.

I keep scrolling through the search results. I was on the news that night, too. I watch the news clip where an anchorman introduces the story about the missing four-year-old girl that police are searching for. They show video of the helicopters they used to try to find me, the helicopters I hid from. The anchorman says the girl was later found outside alone in the middle of the night.

Then it cuts to a reporter who interviews the woman who says the little girl came up to her in front of the laundry while she was outside smoking. "She was absolutely frozen," the woman says, clearly angry. "That baby was a block of ice, I tell you. I don't know what kind of mother would have their child outside like that. No coat. No shoes. That's wrong."

Seeing her now, she looks familiar. At the time there was something about her face that made me think she was safe to talk to, so I walked up to her in front of that laundromat and told her I was cold. She looked like a mother to me, and I knew she would treat me okay.

And she did. She brought me inside right away, where it was brightly lit and warm. She took a blanket from her laundry basket and wrapped it around me. It was still warm from the dryer and smelled like lavender.

The woman said, "You must be that little girl everyone's looking for. You're safe now."

I remember that feeling.

Now, in the computer room, I play another video clip that has to be from earlier that night, before I was found. On the screen, I see an older woman, light skinned with freckles across her nose and cheeks. I sit up straighter. I know her. *I remember the way she used to hug me and tell me how much God loved me.*

Across the screen it reads: *Yvette Singleton, babysitter.*

I feel a tingling in my face watching her talk about me. Mother Singleton. From the church.

"Her family was in Richmond for a funeral, and I was baby-sitting her. Her uncle came home around ten, ten-fifteen, and that precious baby was in her bed, sleep, when I left." She shakes her head, obviously worried about me. "I don't know what could have happened. I hope she wasn't taken out that house by someone. Kidnapped. Oh Lord."

I can see the fear in her eyes and feel her fear through the screen, even though I know how it all turned out. I wasn't kidnapped. But still, I feel bad that she had to live through that. I know she prob-ably felt guilty for leaving me even though she didn't do anything wrong. She didn't know what was going on in that house.

Anyway, everything that happened after she left me there was my fault, even when Grandma threw us out. That was my fault, too.

I'm the one who left.

There's not a lot I remember about that night. Except the anger. The shouting. The chaos.

We were back home, at Grandma's house, and I was scared. And tired. I was still in the nightgown I left home in, and Mom had me in her arms, tight.

And I was crying, trying to hide my face in her neck. I didn't want to see him.

Mom was screaming, "You let a four-year-old leave the house by herself? What's the matter with you, Raymond?"

I remember her hand on my back, rubbing up and down, warming me. She was crying, too, saying, "Do you know what could have happened to her? My baby was out on the streets by herself because of you."

"I didn't do anything!" Raymond shouted back. "How was I supposed to know she would walk out like that?"

"She's four!" Mom screamed back. "Four!" Pressed against her, I could feel her heart beating hard and fast. "You're blaming a four-year-old? What's wrong with you?"

Grandma was there, too, telling Mom to calm down, telling Uncle Raymond to apologize, telling everyone to stop. Stop. Stop.

I don't remember how it all ended. I just remember that was the last time I was ever inside Grandma's house. There was crying after that, and lots of anger, and long stretches of quiet. And there was nobody to play with. It was just us two. Me and Mom.

We never talked about Grandma or Uncle Raymond. But I knew, all that fear and screaming and crying—it was all because of me.

· · · · ·

I'm still there in the computer room, staring at my screen, when the door opens and Jarrett comes in.

"Oh, Caprice. Sorry. I just wanted to check the cartoon one more time before I show it. Just to, you know, make sure it's . . . Are you—do you want privacy?"

"No." I'm reading another article about what happened, and by now I've lost count of how many I already read. I'm reading the articles written the next day now, when the newspaper reporters were trying to wrap everything up, make it seem like there was a happy ending to the missing child story.

Of course, they don't write about how my family fell apart that night.

Jarrett sits at the next computer, and a few minutes later, his cartoon is on the screen. "Want to hear how it sounds with your voice?"

I turn my attention away from my screen. "Huh?"

He points to my screen. "Is that you when you were a kid? That's definitely you."

"Yeah, I'm just trying to research and, like, remember stuff."
"Oh."

Me and Jarrett's eyes meet, and I give him a smile. "I'm sorry," I tell him. "I just have a lot on my mind."

He looks back at the screen. "You were *missing*?"

I nod. "When I was a little kid. Four. In Baltimore."

"Your parents must have been . . ."

"Yeah, they were." The silence kinda hangs in the air. It feels too sad, so I say, "Show me the cartoon!"

While I watch Jarrett and Ennis's little movie, I laugh and laugh. It's so cute. And it's fun watching my voice coming outta that adorable little sewer rat. "I love it!" I tell him, and I really mean it. "It's gonna be the hit of the festival!"

"I hope so. I'm kinda nervous."

"Don't be. It's really great."

But even as I tell him not to be nervous, I'm feeling a little nervous, too. I have to read my poem to a crowd of people. First time I've ever done that.

Me and Jarrett talk while we log off our computers and get ready to go to the festival. We walk outta the computer room holding hands and laughing.

The second we step into the hallway, we see his mom near the front doors with Jarrett's little sister, Treasure, and the baby strapped in one of those baby holder things. His mom is standing there talking to *my* mom. We drop each other's hands fast.

Treasure runs over to Jarrett and jumps into his arms. He tickles her a little and then puts her down, but she grabs his hand tight.

"Caprice," Mom says, "something's come up. We need to go. Now."

"What? Why?"

"It's Grandma, baby." Mom's voice cracks a little.

"Did she—?"

"No, no. But she suffered complications. It's serious. We need to get to Baltimore. I have your suitcases and everything you need."

"But—" I can't believe this. "I have to read my poem."

"I'm sorry, but we need to get going."

"I forgot something," I say, and turn and go back into the computer room before she can say no.

Jarrett follows me. "You lose something?"

"No, I—" I feel like I'm gonna cry.

"You're shaking." Jarrett puts his hand on my arm. "What's wrong?"

I blow out air over and over, just trying to keep myself from sinking. Then I tell Jarrett I'm okay. "I just. I have to go, and I won't be back. I mean, not until, like, Thanksgiving and winter break."

Jarrett nods. "Okay, I mean, I thought you would be here for the weekend, but . . ." He takes my hand again. "Can I text you while you're away?"

I smile. "Definitely." I give him a hug and whisper, "I really like you, but I have a lot going on and, like, I don't know if I'm ready for—"

"I know," he says, still holding me tight. "I like you a lot, too. And when we're ready, maybe me and you can . . ."

"Yeah," I say, pulling away and looking him in the face. "Think we can be friends?"

"How about friends-plus?" he says.

"I like that. Friends-plus."

To be honest, friends-plus is about all I can handle.

complications

it's not just grandma's health.
there are complications
everywhere
with everyone.

me and nicole
have complications.
we are changing
and moving apart.
our friendship isn't easy
the way it used to be.

me and jarrett
have complications.
we have feelings
for each other, but
i may never be ready
for more than that.

me and mom
have complications, too.
we are close, but
i can't tell her
the truth, and now
with grandma's complications
i may never get the chance

On the way outta the Center, I'm practically begging Mom to change her mind, at least when it comes to me. "I can stay with Nicole," I say. "Dad can pick me up from there and take me back to Ainsley."

Mom doesn't slow down as she heads toward the car. "You told me she canceled the sleepover. She has other plans."

"Yeah, but—Mrs. Valentine won't let me be stranded."

"You're not stranded. And I wouldn't feel comfortable leaving you in Newark alone. You belong with me, with your family, at a time like this."

"But . . ."

I stop talking when I see Mom wipe the tears that have sprung into her eyes. She's actually crying. Seeing this almost breaks me.

The last time I saw Mom cry was when Dad was away and things weren't going well between them. They were talking about splitting up. Then one night, right after dinner, Mom actually broke down and cried right there at the kitchen table, right in front of me. She said her heart felt like ice.

That's what mine feels like now. Ice that's cracking into a million pieces.

We get in the car, Mom in the front and me in the back. Then she turns around and says, "Your grandmother, she needs surgery. It's going to be tough for her, but her kidneys . . . There's no choice. I need to be there with her. I don't know. It feels like I have to do this."

Mom looks so scared. It's hard to see her like this. But what she's saying is true. If Mom was the one who was sick, there's no way I could stay away. No matter what she did to me.

I lean forward and wrap my arms around her as best I can. I don't wanna go back there, to that house, to everything it's gonna do to me to be there, but I have to go with her.

Mom needs me.

• • • • • •

A little while later, I wake up from a nap and look out the window at the endless highway. Mom is driving too fast. She's not crying anymore, and she's trying to sing along to the radio, but her voice is cracking.

I can tell when someone else is struggling.

"Mom," I say. "Slow down."

"Yeah, you're right. I'm sorry. I just want to get there."

I lean back in my seat as the car slows down a little. "Did you tell Dad you're bringing me to Baltimore?"

"I just talked to him. He's not happy, but he knows there's no choice."

I wonder if they got into an argument about it. But that's not really what's on my mind. "Who's gonna be there, at Grandma's house?"

As Mom lists the names of the family who live in Baltimore and others who might come in from other places, the only name I'm waiting to hear is Uncle Raymond's. But she doesn't mention him. Maybe the army didn't let him leave Germany.

Maybe I don't need to be scared.

"I know what we need," I tell Mom and pull out my phone. I connect it to the Bluetooth and search for a playlist that has the two words I know will cheer her up: *Boy Bands.* Then I hit play on Boy Bands of the '80s, '90s & Today.

The first song that comes on is "Candy Girl" by some group named New Edition. I never heard of them, but Mom actually gasps. "Oh my God! This is an oldie but goodie." And right away she's singing along to some of the dumbest lyrics I've ever heard. But it's fun watching her.

As the songs play, I sing to some of the newer stuff, and I have to say, the drive goes a lot faster this way. There are long minutes that pass where I actually forget where we're going.

• • • • •

Hours later, we're driving through the streets of Baltimore. Mom turns down the Backstreet Boys as we pass block after block of three-story row houses with red or tan or gray bricks, all attached together. Some have flower boxes in the window, which are really pretty.

I don't remember any of this.

We keep driving, and the neighborhood changes. There are no buildings here, just a bunch of one-family houses that all look different. And as the car drives through these blocks, I'm remembering.

I remember the cold, the little slapping sounds my bare feet made when they hit the cold concrete. I remember wishing I had put on my favorite fuzzy robe and my Winnie the Pooh slippers.

The car gets closer to the corner where the laundromat was, and when we get close enough, I see that it's still there. The 24-Hour Wash & Fold. It looks the same, too.

We get closer to where Grandma lives. *I remember cars coming down the street, their headlights coming close to shining on me. I hear the whir of a helicopter.*

I see a narrow house up ahead, and I know it's the one. "That's Grandma's house," I say, almost to myself.

Mom laughs. "You couldn't forget that house."

And it's true. Grandma's house stands out, even from the others on the block, which are tan or white or brown. Grandma's house is a faded blue. It has a slanted roof and an awning that's a little crooked. The only thing that's different is the yard in front. It's just dirt and weeds, no flowers.

Grandma always had a garden. I wonder when that changed.

When she got sick.

We pull up and park on the side of the house, and before we can even get outta the car, the front door opens and a woman comes running out.

She's a tall, curvy woman with big hair and bright lipstick. Now that I see her, I know who she is because her face reminds me of Grandma. They're sisters.

Mom gets out of the car and gets wrapped up in her aunt's arms. Then, because I don't want her to think I'm being rude, I get out and let her hug me, too. "No way is this Caprice!" Aunt Gwen says, looking at me and then pulling me back to her and holding me there. "Lord, I can't tell you how I prayed for the day I could hold you again."

I can feel how much she missed me. And how happy she is that I'm back. So I relax and let Aunt Gwen love me.

A short time later, Mom gives me a kiss and says. "I need to get over to the hospital for a meeting with Grandma's doctors. You'll be okay here?"

I nod. In a way, I'm happy she doesn't wanna take me with her to the hospital. I don't think I can deal with any of that.

But when she leaves, I'm there with Aunt Gwen alone, and I don't really know what to say. We have dinner, and after I'm stuffed full of Aunt Gwen's baked chicken with rice, she asks me a bunch of questions about school and the summer program and all of that.

"Look at you," she says. "Your grandma is going to be so proud when she hears all you've been up to."

I remember that about her. Grandma would call me her little one and say things like: "My little one knows all her letters!"

It made me feel so good back then.

Aunt Gwen starts clearing dishes from the table, and I get up to help, but she says, "You go relax. I got this."

"But—"

Aunt Gwen points to the living room. "Go on. I'll be in there in just a few minutes." She puts my plate in the sink.

I go into the living room and look around while I wait. Everything still looks the same. The shelves are still there and so are the glass dolls. Only now they're not as high up as I remember. The dolls are beautiful. No wonder I always wanted to play with them.

I look around the rest of the living room, at all the family pictures on the wall. There's a bunch of pictures of Mom: getting some trophies, graduating from high school and college, Mom and

Dad's wedding picture. We have one just like it at home.

There are pictures of Mom and Uncle Raymond, too, when they were young. I remember those pictures. But now I just move past them.

"You want anything else to eat?" Aunt Gwen calls out from the kitchen. "I have some macaroni salad. And cornbread."

"No, thanks," I say. "I'm full."

I hear the water turn on, and while she washes dishes, I find myself moving across the room. It's a feeling. It's like I wanna stay away from the basement door, but I can't stop myself from turning the doorknob. I have to see it. Like, I need to know that my memories are real. That they belong to this house.

I walk down a few of the carpeted stairs slowly and quietly, almost like the little girl in me is afraid Uncle Raymond is still here. I can't go all the way down though. There's something about touching the floor with my feet that will make me feel like I'm back for real, and I don't know if I can do it. So I sit on the stairs and try to breathe.

The basement is dark, but it's better this way. I don't wanna see everything. What I can make out is enough. For now.

The side of the basement with the washing machine and dryer is still exactly the same. Even the folding table is still in the corner, with all the detergents and fabric softener on a metal shelf on top of it.

But the other side, the side that used to be Uncle Raymond's room, everything is different. There are no posters on the wall, no TV, no PlayStation.

The bed is gone.

Now that side of the room is just storage. Junk. Stuff in boxes, an exercise bike with the pedals missing, a ton of magazines in boxes. There used to be a lot of empty space. It seemed so big down here when I was a kid. I remember that's what I used to love about the basement. There was so much room, and there wasn't anything down here I could break.

Down here in the basement, Uncle Raymond would hold my hands and spin me around so fast my feet would lift off the ground. I would call it flying. Sitting here now, I can hear my little voice begging, "Make me fly again, Uncle Raymond. Higher this time!"

I try to breathe. Just breathe. But I feel like I'm gonna be sick.

I can make you fly high to the sky if you play with me first.

I was too young to get it then, but staring into the empty, dark basement, I see what he did. He got me to love him. Trust him. He made me laugh.

Then he hurt me.

So much happened down here. It's too hard to think about. So I try not to think. I sit and stare into the dark room and breathe again. And again.

It takes me a few minutes to realize I'm crying.

No matter what I do, I can't stop thinking about it. My body remembers. My body hurts.

I wanna move, get up, and run outta the house, but I can't.

There's nowhere to go.

It's Aunt Gwen who finds me there on the steps. The open basement door sheds light on the stairs and the basement, and now I see the shelf of army men *are* still there.

"Here you are," she says, coming down the stairs. "The family is here, and everybody wants to see you."

I wipe my face fast. Try to pull myself together before she sees me. But I can't.

Aunt Gwen sits next to me on the step. "You okay?"

I shake my head.

She puts her arm around my waist. "All of this is hard, I know. Your grandmother has good doctors. They're doing everything they can. I was there at the hospital today, and she's holding on."

I feel myself sinking. All those memories are pulling me inside them.

"Come on, Caprice. It's time to meet your family again."

We stand up and walk upstairs, me in front, Aunt Gwen's hand on my back. She's not Grandma. I know that. But her hand feels close to the real thing.

never

he never grabbed me
he never slapped me
he never kicked me
he never punched me
he never threw me down
he never threatened me
he never left bruises on my body
he never forced me to do anything
he never needed to

Upstairs, the house is full of people I think I know. *Should* know. There's an older couple sitting on the sofa, and a younger woman sitting on the floor with two little boys who I'm guessing are her kids. The boys look maybe five and six, and they're playing Connect Four.

As soon as I step into the living room, the older woman stands up with her arms opened wide. "This is *not* Caprice!" she says.

"Yes, it is," Aunt Gwen says. "I know, right?"

The woman wraps me up in a hug that feels new and familiar at the same time. She's a smaller woman than Aunt Gwen, so I'm not smothered as much, but this woman is crying. "Do you remember me?" she asks, but she doesn't wait for me to answer. "I'm your grandmother's oldest sister, Tishelle."

"Don't cry," I say.

"I lost so much time with you. I wanted to watch you grow. And now you're this beautiful young lady."

I smell her sweet jasmine perfume and feel her strong arms around my body. Now I remember her. Aunt Tish. I remember how she used to fill the church with her voice.

"You sing," I say, still holding on to her. "I remember."

"You know that's right!" Aunt Gwen says from across the room. "My sister don't sing. She *sangs*!"

Everybody laughs. I smile and hold on to Aunt Tish.

"Baby, I ached for you," Aunt Tish whispers. *"Ached."*

I can tell by the way she's holding on to me and not letting me go, she's telling the truth. And I can tell I've had this hug a million times before. It's like one of those things you didn't know you missed until you have it back.

Later in the evening, Mom is still not back from the hospital, so I hang out in the living room with Aunt Gwen, Aunt Tish, her husband, Uncle Bernard, their daughter, Maya, and her two sons, Brian and Matt. It's like a whole family I didn't remember I had. Before I know it, the photo albums come out.

Aunt Tish is sitting next to me on the sofa, and we're flipping through a photo album from when Mom was in kindergarten and first grade. Uncle Raymond is in the pictures, too, but he's so small he doesn't look like the person I remember. "Bernard has home movies, too, if you want to see them, Caprice," Aunt Tish says.

From the floor, Maya holds up her hand. "Don't do it, Caprice! You get my father to pull out those old movies, we'll be here all night!" She laughs.

"Don't listen to them," Uncle Bernard says. "I got movies from way back in the day. Movies of your mother when she wasn't nothing but a bit."

I smile. I wouldn't mind seeing those movies.

Aunt Tish puts her arm around me and says, "Now, what's this about you going off to some fancy boarding school? You some kind of genius?"

I laugh. "Oh, no. Not me!"

"Your mother told me you got a scholarship."

"I did, but I'm not that smart. I just really like school and studying."

"Just like your mother," Aunt Gwen says, standing in the doorway to the kitchen. "She was always so good with them numbers."

"She still is," I say.

Aunt Gwen clears her throat like she's about to make an announcement. "Okay, who wants to help me make some brownies?"

The boys jump up and both of them say "Me!" at the same time. They run into the kitchen.

Maya yells after them, "Wash your hands!"

"I'll help, too," I say, and when I go into the kitchen, Aunt Gwen is looking through Grandma's pantry. I remember that pantry. Grandma kept all the good stuff in there: the chocolate chips and the powdered sugar and my favorite, the sprinkles. I loved when she baked cookies.

I don't get to help with the brownies too much because Mom calls me. "Grandma's in surgery," she tells me. "I got to see her for a few minutes before they took her down."

"Is she gonna be okay?"

"I don't know. I spoke to her doctors, and they're optimistic."

"Good."

She asks me how it's going, and I fill her in on what we're doing. "I hope they didn't pull out those old photo albums," Mom says. "And whatever you do, don't let Uncle Bernard—"

"The home movies?" I'm laughing because now I definitely wanna see them.

"Don't get him started!" Mom says. "That man and those movies!"

Me and Mom talk a little while longer, and she says she's gonna stay at the hospital until Grandma comes outta surgery. She tells me to go to sleep in Grandma's room, and she'll be home soon.

Sleeping in Grandma's room. Just like I used to.

. . . . .

While we wait for the brownies to bake, I sit on a stool in the kitchen, and Aunt Tish comes up behind me and takes my locs outta my ponytail holder. "All this thick, pretty hair. How long you had these locs?"

"Um, like six, seven years."

"You never liked getting your hair done. When you were little, you just see a comb and start crying." She laughs. "One day, we were going to—where was that, Gwen? Silver Springs? I don't remember. We were going to some church picnic or something your grandma was helping to organize, and your hair was standing on top of your head like one of them dolls. What are they called?"

"Trolls," I answer, not 100 percent sure I know how I'm following her train of thought.

"Yeah, them." She's running her fingers through my locs, like she can comb them out if she does this long enough. "If you had seen your hair!" She lets out a longer, *louder* laugh. "I had to practically tackle you to get you to sit on that floor, right over there by that couch, so I could grease that scalp and braid your hair. Girl, you did not make it easy, squirming around like an earthworm!"

I start squirming now, and she swats me on the shoulder. Now I laugh and say, "Mom says I was always tender-headed."

"Tender-headed and *bad*!"

My mouth flies open. "Me?"

"Yes, you! Always doing what you wanted. Never listening. Always thinking you were smarter than everybody."

"That doesn't sound like me."

Aunt Gwen hmphs. "Sounds like you to me."

I let Aunt Tish play with my hair for a little while. She makes three flat twists on the top and holds them back with rubber bands. Then she leaves the back out. "There. Now you look like a teenager."

"I'm only twelve."

"Don't get smart with me, missy!"

Everyone laughs, and I have to say, now that I'm back here,

hearing Aunt Tish's voice and seeing how Aunt Gwen smiles to herself while she cooks, and how Maya loves being around her family, I realize I needed this all these years. I needed them.

My family.

· · · · · ·

When it gets dark, I go through one of my suitcases, just to find something to sleep in, and Aunt Gwen walks me upstairs to Grandma's room. She turns the light on and asks me if I need anything.

"I'm okay," I say.

She hugs me for the millionth time. "Every time I think about that night when we almost lost you . . ." She pulls me in even closer. "God was looking out for you that night."

Me and Aunt Gwen say good night, and I close the door behind her. That's when I lose it. I sit on Grandma's bed and cry. Only I'm not sure if I'm crying because I'm happy or sad, because I'm kinda feeling both.

the truth

everybody thinks
uncle raymond lost me.
but he didn't.
i wasn't lost.

i hid.

• • • • •

Grandma's room is exactly the same as I remember it. Everything. The light blue paint is the same, and so is the bedspread. It's beige with faded blue roses. The room even smells the same, like a combination of Avon Skin So Soft and the pink stuff Grandma always puts in her hair at night.

Over the bed there's the big photo of Grandma and Grandpa when they got married. They were standing in front of a church. Smiling. Holding hands. They were both so happy.

In the picture, Grandma looks so pretty, wearing a white wedding dress that shows off all her curves. Grandpa looks a little older. He's in a black suit, looking so handsome with his afro and sideburns. It was winter, but they were outside with no coats on. They were probably not even feeling the cold. That was how in love they were.

I don't remember Grandpa. He died when I was too young. All I know is it was some kind of accident when he was at work, at a loading dock, I think.

Even though he had been gone a long time, when I was little, Grandma only slept on her side of the bed. And Grandpa's stuff was still everywhere. His night table was on the side of the bed near the window, and his watch was still on it. It was large and silver. When I was little, I was scared of it because it had links that would pinch the skin on my arm whenever I tried it on.

And there was Grandpa's shiny lighter, his reading glasses, his Swiss Army knife, and even his wallet. It was one of those leather wallets that folded over and clipped all his credit cards and business cards in place. I probably looked through that wallet a thousand times when I was little. There wasn't any money in it, but there was still a lot of interesting things, like a picture of him from when he was in the army, and some coupons for coffee and cans of Spam and pork and beans.

Now, as I look around the room, seeing all his stuff still there on that night table, still in the same place, I miss him. Someone I never really knew.

I sit on the bed, on Grandma's side, and feel the indentation. That's where she was sleeping that night, when I woke up. I wanted her to get up and open the door for me, but she wouldn't wake up. She was sleeping so hard, and she had that weird mask covering her face. I was scared. I couldn't wake her up, and I was embarrassed. I'd had an accident in her room, and I didn't know how I was gonna face her after what I'd done to her carpet.

I look down now at the light blue carpet, and there's nothing there. No trace of what I'd done. The following morning, Grandma had gotten down on her hands and knees and scrubbed the rug clean with vinegar and water. Then she sprinkled baking soda over the spot until it dried.

Even though I waited for her to say something to me, to tell me I was too old to pee on myself like that, she never said a word to me about it. But after that, she always made me go to the bathroom right before bed.

•––•••––•

After I get dressed for bed, I go down the hall to the bathroom, and on the way back, I open the door to the yellow bedroom that used to be mine, just to see it again. Back when I lived here, I shared a room with Mom since Dad was always away.

Mom worked late a lot back then, and sometimes I was asleep before she came home. I would be in that room all by myself. Lonely. Unless Uncle Raymond sneaked in, or got me to sneak out with him.

Standing in the doorway now, I see Brian and Matt sleeping on the full-size bed. My bed. But nothing in this house is mine. Not anymore. It's like I'm a stranger here.

Actually, even when I lived here, I stopped sleeping in my bed when I started sleeping with Grandma. This stopped being my room a long time ago.

I go back to Grandma's room, turn off the light, and get in bed on Grandpa's side. But I can't sleep. It's like everything is swirling around in my head. This was a long day.

I'm half asleep, half awake, and I remember what Grandma said the first time she brought me in here to sleep with her. She said sleeping with her would keep me safe. Safe from what? Safe from who?

I sit up in bed and stare into the darkness.

She knew.

She had to know what was happening. All those times she told Uncle Raymond to stop playing with me. All those times she would swat him away from me and tell him, "Leave that baby alone." *She knew.* That's why she brought me in here to sleep with her every night.

Like it only happened at night.

Grandma knew what Uncle Raymond was doing to me, but she didn't stop it. She didn't tell my mom or dad. She kept quiet and let it keep happening. Grandma didn't save me because the person hurting me was her son.

She picked him over me.

I lie back down, crying silently, with my chest feeling like there's a boulder on it. It's hard to breathe. My grandmother didn't protect me. I'm here thinking she loved me, and maybe she did, but she didn't love me as much as her son.

And now I'm angry. More than angry. I'm burning. I wanna scream. It's like I don't know what to think or what to feel.

It's too much. It's too much for me to deal with.

I need to get outta this room.

I get outta bed and go out into the hall, tears still streaming down my face. I can hear the adults downstairs, still talking, but I don't want them seeing me like this. So I go back in the room, grab my phone, and go into the bathroom.

I sit on the floor and call Mom, but it goes right to voice mail. She probably has it turned off. I try to take the shakiness outta my voice so I can leave a message and not make her worry. "Mom, I just wanted to see if you were coming home soon. I'm okay. Wake me up when you get here." I swallow hard and add, "I'm okay."

I click the phone off and break down again. It hurts. It really hurts. Nobody looked out for me. Even the one person who knew what was happening.

I'm still holding the phone, and I need someone to talk to and it's a weird feeling, but I'm nervous calling Nicole. Not because it's late but because I don't know if she's gonna wanna talk to me. I don't know if she's finished with me.

It takes three rings before she answers, and at first I'm not sure if it's the voice mail or Nicole because her voice is flat when she says, "Hello." She's never answered the phone like that with me. Never that cold.

"It's, um . . . It's . . ." I can't stop crying. "It's me."

Silence.

"I'm—I'm sorry for missing your dance. At the festival. I . . ." All of a sudden I don't know why I called her. What did I even wanna say to her?

Finally, Nicole says something. "Jarrett and Ennis's cartoon was really funny. I heard your voice."

I wipe my tears. "I never thought my first acting role would be sewer rat."

Nicole laughs a little. "You were cute."

I move the phone away from my face for a few seconds so she won't hear me crying. Then I breathe in hard and say, "I wish we were talking yesterday because after Woman Group, me and Jarrett kissed."

Nicole actually squeals. "Oh. My. God."

"But I couldn't call you because we're not friends anymore."

"I didn't say that."

We're quiet again. Then I say, "I'm sorry. I—"

"You don't need to apologize for any—"

"Yeah, I do. I do. You kept asking me if I was okay, and . . ." I break down and cry way too loud to hide it from Nicole anymore.

"Are you crying?" Nicole asks.

"You were right. I'm not okay. I'm . . ." I'm crying so hard now, I have to suck in air like a little kid.

"Come on. Don't cry, Caprice."

I'm trying, but it takes a bunch of minutes before I can stop.

It's like my chest is full of pain, and the pressure is choking me.

"Where are you?" she asks. "Where's your mom?"

"I'm in Baltimore, at my grandma's house. Mom is—"

"Is your grandma okay? She didn't die, did she?"

"No, no. She's alive. She had to have an operation."

"Oh, I hope she's okay."

"Me too." Thinking about Grandma makes me feel that pain in my chest again. I have too many feelings. Sadness, worry, anger, all directed at Grandma. I don't know what to do with them all. "That's not why I'm crying."

Nicole's voice is much softer when she says, "You know you can talk to me. And this time I won't tell anyone. I promise."

I wipe my tears.

"Seriously," she says. "You can trust me."

I lift my head up and look at the ceiling while I try to let her words sink in. I hope I *can* trust her because I can't do this alone anymore. I need her.

And for the next hour, sitting there on the bathroom floor, in between crying out loud and crying to myself, I tell Nicole everything. I tell her about when I used to live here, and how my dad was always away with the Marines, and Mom was always working, and I wanted Uncle Raymond to be my friend and let me hang out with him. "But there was always, like . . . He always wanted something from me. I had to do things to him and let him do things to me."

I hear Nicole gasp. "Oh no," she whispers.

"I was just a little kid. I didn't know, I . . ."

"He's the one who did the wrong thing, Caprice. Not you."

"I know. It's just hard to . . . I always remembered what he did, even when I was a little older, but I didn't understand it. Like, I didn't know what it was for until I got old enough to understand what sex was and all that, and now I know what he was doing and it makes me sick. I can't hold this in anymore. It makes me feel disgusting, like I didn't even have a choice. He took all my choice away." I'm rocking back and forth.

"You didn't do anything wrong," Nicole says again. "He's the one who's disgusting, not you. You were just a little girl." Now I hear that she's crying, too. "Nobody should have done that to you. It wasn't right."

Both of us stop talking for a long time, and all I hear is crying and sniffling through the phone. Then Nicole asks, "Is your uncle there now?"

"No, I'm not sure if he's gonna make it. He's in the army, and it's hard for him to come back."

"Good."

"I know."

"You have to tell your mom and dad," Nicole says. "They have to know."

"Grandma's too sick. I can't—"

"You have to tell them. Promise me you'll tell them."

I let out a deep breath. "I'll tell them tomorrow," I say. "As soon as I'm back at Ainsley."

"So you're definitely going?"

"Yeah." Then, after a few seconds of quiet, I say, "Just because I'm going away, you know that doesn't mean we're not still best friends. No matter what, you're always gonna be my best friend."

"I know," she says. "And you'll always be mine. I wanna talk to you every day, even if it's just for a few minutes."

"Me too," I say. "And I still wanna have sleepovers whenever I'm home. I mean, I wanna do it until we're way too old for sleepovers, like when we're thirty-three."

We both try to laugh but end up sniffling. There are still too many tears in the way.

"Everything's gonna be different now," Nicole says. I can't tell if she's sad or if she's just realizing this.

"Yeah, I know." Me and her get quiet again.

Then Nicole says, "Try to fall sleep, okay? And call me if you need help telling your parents."

"I will."

We say good night and hang up, and I stay on the bathroom rug for a long time. Then I pick myself up and go back to Grandma's room. And I wait till Mom comes back.

· · · · ·

In bed, my brain is like a tornado, storming and swirling and keeping me awake. I'm thinking about Grandma's operation, meeting my family, telling Nicole the truth, leaving for Ainsley tomorrow, all of it at the same time.

Every time I close my eyes, I'm remembering.

I remember being in the basement with Uncle Raymond, and Grandma stomping down the stairs and pulling me back upstairs with her. She told me, "You stay up here with me. I want to see you at all times!"

I remember being in bed with Grandma, and waking up, hearing whispering. "Caprice, Caprice." It was Uncle Raymond, whispering with the door cracked open just a little. "I have a surprise for you." And I remember getting outta bed and tiptoeing to the door, quiet so Grandma wouldn't wake up.

I was so stupid.

I remember Grandma catching Uncle Raymond one time. He opened the door and whispered my name, only this time, Grandma was still awake. She jumped outta bed and slapped Uncle Raymond in the face and on his arm and back as he ran away. She told him he was sinful.

She said that.

I remember Grandma taking me to the bathroom every night right before we went to bed. Then she brought me in this room, and she locked the door behind us.

A lock.

Now I practically jump outta bed and turn the light back on. I race to the door, and there's no lock, but there is a little metal bracket on the doorframe, like the kind one of those locks would slide into. And when I look closer, there are four indentations in the wood on the door, like where the screws were. Only now, the holes have been covered up with some kind of wood stain. They're hard to see.

My memory was right. There *was* a lock on this door. Grandma made me sleep with her when Mom was working late, but Uncle Raymond still got to me. Then she locked me in. That was why I couldn't open the door the night I had the accident.

I get back in bed, but I'm still too upset to fall asleep. Grandma knew what was happening, but instead of stopping it, all she did was lock me in her room. And *that* didn't even work. I still ended up alone with Uncle Raymond the last night I lived here.

I cry myself to sleep, and when I wake up in the middle of the night, Mom is asleep next to me. I don't know when she got there, but I'm glad she is. At least I'm not here in this room alone with my memories anymore.

In the morning, I wake up to Mom's voice on the phone. I can tell she's talking to someone from the hospital.

"How's Grandma?" I ask when she clicks the phone off.

"She's still asleep. And she's weak. We're going to church to pray for her, pray she wakes up."

I get outta bed, but I'm moving in slow motion. That's how tired I am. At least I'm not crying anymore.

I search through my suitcases for a dress, sandals, and the one and only purse I'm bringing to Ainsley. And once I'm dressed, I go downstairs and help Aunt Gwen cut up the green peppers and onions for the omelettes she's making for everyone.

Aunt Tish and Uncle Bernard went home last night, but Maya and the boys stayed over. So breakfast is really fun with so many people there. It's like being part of a big family.

Driving to Grandma's church, I look out the window at all the neighborhoods we pass, all the houses and schools and shopping centers. It's all really beautiful. Baltimore is different than the way I remembered it. Or maybe it's me that's changed.

That's probably it.

The church is just the way I remembered it. I used to like to hold Grandma's hand when we came here because it made me feel special to be her granddaughter. Thinking about that now makes me smile.

We get there early, way before the service starts, and all I hear is people calling my mom's name.

"Anita? Nita Charles?"

"Is that you, Nita?"

"I know that ain't Anita Charles?"

Mom laughs and tells everyone, "I'm Anita Barnes now, but yes, it's me." And there's a lot of hugging and laughing and catching up. Then when they see me, it's the same thing. Nobody can believe how big I am.

The thing is, Mom is so happy and so comfortable here, which makes sense since she spent her whole childhood in this church. Before I know it, she's helping the other ladies set up tables with bagels and cake, and then she's pouring coffee for some of the older people.

While Mom talks to everyone, I look around the church. It's not one of those huge megachurches, but it's pretty big. And really nice inside. I'm looking at all the stained-glass windows when I see a woman sitting in the front row, slightly to the right of the altar. She's reading a Bible with her head tilted to the side.

I know her. Mother Singleton. She still looks the same as she did in that old news clip.

And now I remember. She used to babysit for me a lot. She would pick me up from my day-care center in the afternoon and bring me to her house. Then Grandma would pick me up from there when she got off work.

I would only stay with Mother Singleton for a little while, just enough time for her to make me some peanut butter crackers or apples cut into little sticks. Sometimes she gave me raisins, and she didn't mind that I would line them up and play with them on the table. And she had a cute little dog. I forgot his name, but he never bit me, no matter how many times I'd pull on his ear. He was patient with kids.

I loved Mother Singleton.

I walk over and sit next to her in the pew. "Hello," I say, looking at her face full of freckles. "I'm—"

"I know exactly who you are, Caprice," she says, and the way she looks at me with the hint of a smile, I can't help but feel the love she still has for me. She puts her arms around me and hugs me. "You were my favorite little baby. So smart and so kind."

I close my eyes and let her hug me.

Mother Singleton whispers, "This is what I wanted to do to you ever since that terrible night we lost you. I never got to see you again." She sighs long and hard.

I wanna tell her I'm sorry, that it was my fault, that I'm the reason she was so worried. But I don't. It's over now.

She lets me go, but grabs hold of one of my hands. "You know, your grandmother and I had a big falling out after that night. She blamed me for leaving you with your uncle. But I thought everything would be okay. I thought he was responsible enough to keep an eye on you. But . . ." She shakes her head. "I was wrong."

"Did you ever get to be friends with Grandma again?"

"Oh yeah. We're like sisters, the two of us. Nothing could tear us apart for long."

"I have a best friend like that, too."

Mother Singleton kisses me on the forehead. "Your grandma was just trying to look out for you. That's all she wanted."

I nod and say, "I know."

But sitting here now, I really don't know anything. I still don't understand.

I remember that night, waking up in my own bedroom with Uncle Raymond standing over me. "Where's Mother Singleton?" I asked him.

"She went home," he said. "It's just you and me."

I asked him when Mom and Grandma were coming home, and he told me they just left Richmond, and they wouldn't be back for two or three hours.

That felt like a long time to me, and I remember feeling scared. I had never been home alone with Uncle Raymond. Grandma was always upstairs, even if she was sleeping. But now there was nobody here to save me.

Uncle Raymond said, "I have a surprise for you. Do you want to see it?"

Most of the time I would have wanted to see it, but not that night. I just wanted Mother Singleton back.

"If you want to see it, come down to the basement. You're gonna love it, and you can play with it all night."

I remember the way he smiled when he said that because it made me feel trapped.

I felt like that little mouse.

I jumped outta bed and ran down the hall to the bathroom, and I locked the door even though I'd never done that before. Then I just stood there until I heard Uncle Raymond say, "When you're finished, come downstairs for the surprise."

I didn't say anything. I just listened to him going downstairs, and I waited a few more minutes just to be sure he was gone. Then I opened the bathroom door and peeked outside.

I don't remember why, but I tiptoed down the stairs as quietly as I could. But I didn't go to the basement. Instead, I opened the front door, walked outside into the night, and pulled the door closed behind me. I *don't remember where I was going. Maybe I was looking for Mother Singleton, or I wanted to be outside when Mom and Dad got back. I'm not sure.*

But it was cold outside, and I didn't want Uncle Raymond to find me, so I walked away, and I kept walking. And walking. Even when I heard Uncle Raymond calling my name, looking for me, I didn't turn back. I didn't even slow down.

Church lasts a long time, and leaving takes even longer. On the way out, Mom calls the hospital again and finds out Grandma is still asleep, so she decides to take me to the Inner Harbor for lunch. Aunt Gwen and Aunt Tish decide to go straight to the hospital, and Maya and her boys need to go home, so it's just me and Mom.

I'm glad we go, though. Last night was hard, and I'm still tired. Drained. It's like I can't stop my brain from spinning, trying to make sense outta everything. And it's nice here. I don't remember ever being here, but I love it. We walk around the harbor and look at all the boats and tourists and everything.

I wanna tell Mom. I have to. But I can't figure out how. And when.

"You've never had real Maryland crab cakes," Mom tells me, looping her arm around mine. "You better be hungry!" She looks so happy as she pulls me toward a restaurant with a huge crab sign on the roof.

"Starving," I say. And suddenly, I realize I am. Not just for the crab cakes, even though I know they're gonna be amazing. I'm hungry for this. Time together. Dad's catching a flight straight to Baltimore, and it's probably just gonna be me and him driving up to Ainsley. So I wanna make the most of this time with Mom before I leave.

And, yeah, I know I have to tell her, but I don't have to do it now and mess this up. I can tell her later.

·····

After lunch, which was as yummy as I knew it would be, Mom calls the hospital again, and when she gets off the phone, she says,

"They're concerned that Grandma still hasn't woken up. We need to get there now."

At the hospital, Mom grabs my hand as we make our way off the elevator onto the eighth floor. We pass the nurses' station and head down the hall, past glass rooms with beds that are either half or completely surrounded by blue curtains. And there are people in most of the beds, and all of them are hooked up to some type of equipment. It's scary.

I feel myself walk slower, not wanting to get there. It's all too much.

Grandma's room isn't glass. It's a regular room on a hall with other regular rooms. We go in, and Aunt Gwen, Aunt Tish, and Uncle Bernard are already there. They're all sitting in chairs around Grandma's bed. Uncle Bernard looks like he was sleeping until we woke him up, but both of Grandma's sisters have their Bibles open. I think they were reading to her.

It takes me a few seconds to get up the courage to look at Grandma. She's on her back with some kind of mask covering her nose and mouth, like maybe for oxygen to help her breathe. Her eyes are closed, and her skin looks different than the last time I saw her. She used to have beautiful deep brown skin. Now it looks as gray as her hair.

"Grandma . . ." I whisper.

It's her. No matter how much has changed, she's still my Grandma.

"She's sleeping," Mom says. "It's okay. You can get closer to her."

"I don't wanna wake her up," I say. Even after last night and everything I know now, I still love her. And I need to tell her that.

Mom brings me around to the other side of the bed, near the window. She pulls a chair closer to the bed. "Sit down. Talk to her."

I sit, and Mom takes my hand and puts it on top of Grandma's wrist. There's an IV taped to the back of her hand, and I don't want to touch it.

"Grandma?" I say softly. I don't want to startle her. She hasn't heard my voice in so long, maybe it would surprise her too much. "It's me, Caprice."

I look at her face, but it's so still. I actually hold my breath a little.

"Grandma," I say again. "I wanna tell you . . ." I look around the room and everyone is watching me, listening to me. So I just say, "I remember when I lived with you, back when I was a little kid. You always let me grate the cheese for the macaroni and cheese, and remember when you let me put food coloring in, like, everything? We made blue waffles one time!" I laugh, and so does everyone else.

But heaviness wells up in my chest, and it hits me. This could be the last time I get to touch her, talk to her, thank her. What if I never get to hear her voice again, or get a hug from her, or see her look at me with those smiles in her eyes? What if this is the end?

And thick tears spill down my cheeks, and I lower my head, just to let them come. I thought I could hold them back, but now, there's no way. This is too much. Finally, Mom moves her chair next to mine and she takes hold of my other hand. Only now she doesn't tell me everything is gonna be okay.

"Put on some Donnie McClurkin," Aunt Gwen says after a while. "He's one of your grandmother's all-time favorites, Caprice. He's all she plays in her car."

Mom laughs. "And while we did our chores on Saturday morning, that's all she played. Donnie McClurkin. What was the name of that song? The one that was like 'What do you do when some-thing something something?'"

Now it's Aunt Tish who answers. "It's called 'Stand.'" Then she sings it herself, and now I remember her singing voice. It's strong and pretty at the same time. The lyrics are everything I need to hear right now. I need to know that when you don't think you can make it through, you can. *I* can. Every time Aunt Tish sings, "*Child, you just stand*," it brings tears to my eyes.

I cry through the whole song, and Mom rubs my back the whole time. Then she scrolls through her phone and plays some more gospel songs on low volume, just loud enough for Grandma to hear. If she *can* hear anything.

While the music plays, everyone starts telling stories about Grandma, when she did this or that. I sit there, looking at the smiles on everyone's face, listening to the laughs. It's hard to understand how everyone could seem happy at a time like this. It's like they're ignoring what's happening now and trying to remember the good times. It's like a funeral.

Except Grandma is still here.

Alive.

Grandma's hand is big and warm, and my hand still feels small in it. I rub my thumb back and forth in her palm, waiting for her to close her hand around mine, to let me know she feels me there.

But after a while, I have to accept that she doesn't even know I'm here. It feels like a waste of time.

I lean closer to Grandma again. "It's me, Caprice." I whisper right into her ear. "I'm back."

No squeeze. Nothing.

But her hand is still warm and familiar. It reminds me of walking to the store with her, the one down the block and around the corner. It was the store that was across the street from the playground with the twisty slide. Grandma would say we could stop on our way. "But just for three slides," she would say.

Three slides always sounded like a lot until I had slid down twice and I only had one left. "Two more!" I would scream as I ran to the ladder. I was hoping my happiness would make her change her mind and let me get an extra slide.

"No, Caprice," she always said. *Always*. "Last one."

I would climb extra slow, try to take as much time as I could, just to make it last longer. It would probably be a few days or a week before we walked to the store again, and I needed this last slide to satisfy me for that long.

I still remember the feeling of sitting on that hot metal slide and letting go.

I used to let go.

"Grandma," I whisper again now, "remember that slide across the street from the little store where you would buy me chocolate push pops?" Grandma's face is still. "I loved when you took me there. Even though you only let me get three slides."

Across the room, I hear Mom laugh. "She used to do that with me, too."

"Grandma," I say, "that was so much fun."

I don't wanna let go of her hand. Maybe if I keep my hand here long enough, it'll work. She'll feel me. Maybe she missed me. Maybe she'll wanna wake up and hug me.

I rub my hand in a circle on her wrist. "I know you loved me," I tell her. I have questions about a lot of things, but not about that. Never about that.

And that's when I hear, "Nita."

I don't need to look up to know who's come into the room.

Mom stands up and runs over to the door, to hug Uncle Raymond, who is standing there wearing army camouflage. "You made it," she says. "I thought—I didn't think you'd be able to—"

"I thought I had time," he says. "You know how that is. Then the doctor told me she needed surgery and it was serious, and that was all I needed to hear. Got the army to let me leave. Caught the first flight from Germany."

Mom is actually smiling. "Oh my goodness. I'm glad you're here."

But me, I'm holding my breath. I slide the chair away from the bed and try to press myself into the corner of the room, not sure what to do.

I can't be here. I can't do this.

my view
(from the corner)

i watch him hug mom and
aunt tish and aunt gwen and
hold grandma's wrist and
tell her he's there now and
he loves her and
he needs her and
i cry quietly and
hide in the shadow and
try not to be seen and
try not to breathe and
try not to scream.

Suddenly, I stand up and race for the door, but then I feel a hand on my forearm. I stare at it and when I look up, Uncle Raymond has a smile on his face as he holds on to me. "Wow, Caprice. I didn't even recognize you sitting there."

I stare at his face and try to read him. The smile is only in one corner, giving him a crooked look. He's looking at me, but I don't want him to.

"You see how much she's grown?" Aunt Gwen says to him from the other side of the room. "And how beautiful she is."

"Yeah," Uncle Raymond says. "It's been a while, right?"

I hear what he's saying, but I don't like the way he's looking at me. I don't know what it means. I try to pull my arm away from him, but he holds on. "Whoa, Caprice," he says. "Slow down. I want to—"

I know I can't do this. I can't stand here and let him look at me. I can't look at that crooked smile.

From somewhere, I hear a shriek and a "No," and it's in my voice. I finally pull my arm away from him and slip through the door. Fast. And I run down the hall.

There's a waiting area around the corner. I get there and realize I'm not breathing.

I'm sobbing.

I pace around the waiting area, not caring that there are two women sitting there, looking at me with worried-lady faces.

Over and over, I rub the place on my arm where he touched me, where he had the nerve to put his hands on me. The skin there burns. He touched me. He didn't have the right to touch me.

He *never* had the right to touch me.

And it's not fair that he did this to me and got away with it. It's not right.

I can't stop moving and crying and rubbing.

I can't stop burning.

if

if they knew
they wouldn't hug him or rub his back
they wouldn't want to talk to him or touch him
if they knew

if they knew
they wouldn't sit with him or feel sorry for him
they wouldn't want to take care of him or love him
if they knew

they would hate him if they knew

- • - • -

Where is Dad already? Shouldn't he be here by now?

I dig into my backpack for my phone. I had to turn it off for church, and now I see a text from Terra. It's a picture of her mom in a beautiful coral gown for the White House state dinner.

And there's a bunch of missed calls, all from Nicole. I have to call her back, but not now. I'll talk to her after Dad comes and I'm on my way away from here.

Dad answers the phone, and the first thing I say is, "Are you almost here?"

"Just landed and picked up the rental car. Should be there in less than an hour."

"Hurry," I plead, and that's when I realize I'm shaking.

Dad chuckles. "Don't worry. I'll get you to Ainsley tonight. I spoke to the residence hall manager. She said kids arrive all day and night, so it's not a problem."

"Okay. Text me when you get here. I'm in the waiting room."

"Being in Grandma's room was too much for you?" he asks.

"Yeah," I say. "Kinda." My phone vibrates in my hand. I'm getting another call. I look at the phone and see it's Nicole again. "I have to go, Dad."

"Okay, sit tight. I'll be there soon."

I click over to Nicole. "Hello?"

"Caprice?" It's not Nicole.

It's Mrs. Valentine.

"Caprice? Are you there? I've been trying to reach you all morning."

My heart sinks, and I can't speak.

Nicole told.

"Sweetie, I hope you're there. Don't be mad." Mrs. Valentine's voice cracks. "Nicole didn't want to break your confidence, Caprice. She was crying all night. I didn't know what was wrong with her. She wouldn't tell me. She wanted to figure out how to help you on her own, but she was breaking down, so I made her tell me. Don't be mad at her. She didn't know how to handle what you told her."

Now I'm crying quietly. I stand up and walk to the other side of the room, by the window, so the two ladies won't hear me. Meanwhile, Mrs. Valentine is telling me it's okay to cry, that she loves me, that she wishes she could wrap her arms around me.

"Where's your mom, sweetie?"

"In the hospital room with Grandma and my, um, uncle. I'm in the waiting room."

"Oh, dear Lord. Don't go back in there. I can call your mom. I can help you tell her."

"No, no," I say. "Mom's mother is really sick, and she needs to be with her. And I'm leaving. My dad's on the way right now."

"Your mother needs to—"

"Not now, Mrs. Valentine. Grandma just came outta surgery and she needs to wake up and get stronger. My whole family is here supporting her. They're praying and singing, and I don't want to ruin it. I don't want Grandma to die because of me."

"Caprice, I want you to be safe," she says. "I don't want that animal to even look at you."

"Me neither."

"Stay in the waiting room until your dad gets there."

"I will. Don't worry. I'm safe."

I talk to Mrs. Valentine for a few more minutes until she knows for sure I'm okay. Then I say, "Tell Nicole I'm not mad."

After we hang up, I stay there, looking out the window so nobody can see that I'm crying.

What's taking Dad so long?

It's hard to keep my body from shaking. Trembling. I need to get outta here. I need to get away, just like I did the last time I was in Baltimore.

- - - - -

"There you are."

I look up and see Mom standing in the doorway. The two women are still in the waiting room, but now there's another younger woman, too. I didn't even see when she got here.

"Are you okay, baby?" Mom steps into the waiting room and comes over to the window, where I'm still standing. "You didn't come back."

All I can say is, "I'm waiting for Dad."

Mom kisses me on the head. "Seeing Raymond was hard, huh? I can understand that. His irresponsible behavior led to a terrifying night. But he's grown up now. He's a military man, and he lives in Germany. He can't hurt you."

He already did.

Uncle Raymond is right down the hall, and if he comes outta that room, I don't know what I'll do.

Suddenly, everything wells up again, and I need to get outta there. I don't wanna see him.

"I—I want . . . Dad's on the way. He's gonna be here any minute. We need to get to Ainsley."

"Alright. I'm going to say goodbye to everyone so we can leave right away."

"You don't have to come, Mom. Grandma needs you to—"

"I have to make sure you get settled in at school. Dad and I will drive right back tomorrow. Now that Raymond is back, at least someone will always be with her."

"But . . ." Now I feel guilty taking Mom away from Grandma just to bring me back to Ainsley.

That's when Aunt Gwen comes into the waiting room. "Nita, come quick. She's waking up!"

Mom jumps up and grabs my hand. "Come," she says, and she pulls me down the hall and back around the corner with her.

The doctor comes into Grandma's room with us, and while she's examining Grandma, Mom and Aunt Gwen hug each other, and so do Aunt Tish and Uncle Bernard. Nobody's hugging Uncle Raymond, and I'm all the way across the room, standing by the door so he knows not to come near me.

"How are you feeling, Mrs. Charles?" the doctor asks Grandma, putting a stethoscope on her chest. "Are you experiencing any pain?"

Grandma's voice is so low, I can't hear what she says.

But the doctor leans in close to listen, and she says, "Good. Good. Just relax and try to rest."

I wanna go over to Grandma, let her know I'm here, but I'm afraid to move. I don't wanna bring any attention to myself.

Standing there, I know it would be so easy to leave again, to open the door and run out. Running saved my life that night when I was four.

But what if that won't work anymore? What if keeping this inside is too heavy now?

When the doctor finishes examining Grandma and leaves the room, it's then that I notice Grandma's hand is reaching out. For me. I move closer to her bed and I hold her wrist again. But she moves her fingers, so I take her hand as tenderly as I can. "Grandma," I say, "I'm here."

"Caprice," Grandma whispers with a weak smile.

"It's me." I move in close to her so she can see me. And in that short time, her face looks so much better. It's like there's life back in her.

Then Grandma raises her other hand. "It's you," she says, touching my face. "My little one."

Her little one. I love hearing her call me that again.

"I'm . . . sorry," she says.

"No, Grandma. You don't have to be—"

"Caprice." Dad steps into the room. "I thought you were going to be in the waiting room." He goes straight over to Mom to give her a kiss.

"Sorry," I say, wanting to hug him but not wanting to let go of Grandma's hand.

"I brought her back here," Mom says. "Not her fault."

Dad hugs all of Mom's family, and I watch as Uncle Raymond slowly moves away from them, away from Dad, to the corner next to Uncle Bernard.

The big army man is scared of my father.

Aunt Tish and Aunt Gwen come over to the bed and talk to Grandma, and then Mom comes over and leans over to kiss her. "I'm sorry," Grandma tells her, and the way she looks at Mom, it's like she wants to explain herself.

"It's okay, Ma. We can talk about everything later, when you're back home and feeling better."

But Grandma doesn't stop. She whispers, "Anita, I didn't want to . . . I had to."

Mom shakes her head like she doesn't have time for this. "You always have choices," she says, and her face flashes with anger. But she doesn't say anything else. She just turns away, and I can't see her face anymore, but I know she's crying. Finally, Mom says to Dad, "Let's go, Dar."

Grandma tries to sit up in bed, but I press on her shoulders, trying to keep her in place. "No, Grandma. You can't." And now Aunt Tish is by my side trying to help me keep Grandma in bed.

But Grandma is still trying to move. "I have to . . . explain."

"There's nothing to explain," Mom says. "Just stop."

Across the room, Uncle Raymond isn't moving. I stare at him, watching everything. All of this is his fault. He's the reason our whole family is broken apart. Only nobody knows it but me, him, and Grandma, and nobody's letting her explain.

I have to tell.

Maybe it's time. "I know what Grandma wants to say," I tell everyone. "She's trying to tell you why she made us leave."

Everyone's looking at me. Waiting for me to keep talking.

That's when Uncle Raymond says, "I don't know what's going on here, but I didn't fly back from Germany for this." He steps closer to Grandma's bed, closer to me, and it's too much. He's too close. I move away as fast as I can and wrap my arms around Dad. "I wanna go," I tell him. "Let's go."

From across the room I hear Grandma say, "It's . . . okay, Caprice."

Uncle Raymond says, "What's okay?" And now he's sounding and looking nervous.

So I do it. I say, "When I was a little girl, Uncle Raymond touched me and hurt me over and over. I didn't tell anyone because—"

I can't even finish before Dad is practically flying across the room. He grabs Uncle Raymond by the throat and slams him up against the wall. And I'm standing there alone, crying and crying, listening to Uncle Raymond lie and say, "It's not true. It's not true." And Mom is screaming, "Dar, don't kill him. Dar!"

And in the next few minutes, security is in the room and they hold Uncle Raymond until the police get there. And he's arrested. And everyone is crying. And all I can do is go back to Grandma and hold her hand through it all.

⋯ • • • ⋯

In the car, on the highway in the dark, I'm in the back seat somewhere between exhausted and numb. Dad's driving, and I can see Mom's hand on his shoulder. They're not talking, probably because they think I'm sleeping, but the truth is, I'm too tired to sleep.

I close my eyes again and try to rest my mind, but it's hard to stop thinking about everything that happened today, this week.

Especially tonight. I had to tell police officers every terrible thing Uncle Raymond did to me. That was hard. But I did it. And I survived.

And now I don't have to worry anymore about what would happen if I told.

We drive in silence for a long time. We're headed somewhere. Fast.

And that's when it hits me. I don't actually know where we're going. Are we going to Grandma's house? To Ainsley? Or just driving back to Newark?

Part of me wants to know. The other part just wants to go wherever I'm taken. Let someone else decide.

I close my eyes again and try not to feel anything. I lean my head against the door and get as comfortable as the seat belt will let me. A few minutes later, I hear Mom whisper, "How could I not know?"

"How could we *both* not know?" Dad responds.

Mom sighs heavily. "He's my brother. How could he . . . ?"

"I don't . . ."

"Why didn't she . . . ? Why didn't she think she could . . . ?"

"I don't . . ."

There's silence.

I wish I could help them understand me, but I don't know the answer to their questions either. Maybe I just didn't want them to even have these questions. I didn't want them to have to worry about me. I'm not *that* kid that parents worry about. I'm the one they think is always okay.

My chest hurts, but I can't cry anymore. It's like my whole body is empty and sore.

I told. It's outta me. Now I need to know, who will I be without the secret?

My phone vibrates in my pocket. It's Nicole. I called her from the police station, but we couldn't talk long. Now all she texts is:

> im proud of you.

In a little while, I think I'll be proud of me, too.

We pull up in front of a huge hotel, nothing like the cheap one we stayed at when Grandma made us leave. This hotel is fancy.

Mom gets out and comes around to help me out like I'm a little baby. But that's kinda how I feel.

"Why are we here?" I ask. "I thought we were going . . ."

"We need to meet with some investigators from the district attorney's office on Tuesday. So we have to stay here for a couple of days."

I stand there beside the car for a little while, so tired it's hard to keep my knees straight. I've never felt like this before. It's like I'm so drained my body can't move.

I lean against the car, and Mom puts her arm around me and holds me up. But I still can't move. "What about Ainsley?"

Mom runs her hand down the side of my face. "I need more time with you. I can't let you go now. I need to wrap you in my arms for a lot longer."

And that's what she does. We stand there in the hotel parking lot with her arms tight around my shoulders, and I rest my head against her, and I begin to cry. And then Dad is behind me, rubbing my back and telling me, "It's okay. It's okay."

And I wanna believe him. I do. It's gonna be okay. *I'm* gonna be okay. I will.

But I'm not okay now.

"I'm not ready to go away to Ainsley," I finally say. "I can't—"

"Shhh," Mom says. "I'll call them in the morning."

My mind is too full to think.

"I need more time with you," Mom says again. "And Dad and I need to find a counselor for you. Someone who knows how to help you through this."

"Okay," I say, still leaning against Mom. "Dr. Isidro, she said she can help me find a counselor in Newark."

"I'll reach out to her," Dad says.

We're quiet for a few seconds and then I say, "I still wanna go to Ainsley for high school. I really do." And now that I say it out loud, I know it's the right decision.

Because for now, I need to stay and finish middle school with Nicole the way we always planned. I need Mom and Lana and Mrs. Prajapati and Mrs. Valentine, all the women who always supported me. I need them more than I ever did before. I need Newark and the Center and Woman Group and Express Yo'Self.

Basically, I need to be home.

now I know

secrets are heavy to carry
they press on your heart
holding you down

when you release them
secrets float away
light and free
like spring air

Mom and I leave Baltimore in the morning. After Grandma is transferred to a rehabilitation center so she can recover and get stronger. After I've talked to so many people from the district attorney's office and told them everything that happened with Uncle Raymond.

After I've cried so much, there's nothing left.

But still, leaving Baltimore is harder than I ever thought it would be. I spent so many years being scared of this place, but now, all I can think of is when I get to come back. I'm connected to Baltimore. It's family.

And there's still a lot I need to know, to understand. I need to talk to Grandma, hear her explain why she thought she could protect me when she couldn't. Why she never told anyone what was happening. Why she made us leave. Not him.

But she's still too weak. And maybe I am, too.

So I'll have to wait for the right time. When we're both ready.

Just like we did two weeks ago, we drive straight to the Center, even before going home. Nicole and I planned to meet here right after she got outta school because, for some reason, I don't wanna go into the Center alone.

Two weeks ago, when I came back from Ainsley, I felt like I had changed a ton, but that was nothing compared to now. After this week in Baltimore, I feel like an entirely different person.

This is what it feels like to not have secrets.

My phone buzzes in my hand. It's Nicole's text.

> coming down the street.

I text back.

> in mom's car

Then I see her, walking with Ayla and Gina. Nicole looks nice, wearing jeans and a blue-green top I never saw before. I know it's only the second day of eighth grade, but she kinda looks older. More sophisticated. As she gets closer, I see that she's wearing new hoop earrings, too.

I jump outta the car, but even before I can close the door behind me, Nicole is running down the street. She throws her arms around me, and she hugs me so hard and so long, I'm surprised. "I'm so glad you're back," she says. "You don't know how much I missed you!"

"I know," I say, hugging her back just as hard.

Nicole doesn't know how much she helped me this past week. I talked and texted with her day and night, before and after every interview with the prosecutor and the investigators who are gonna try to keep Uncle Raymond locked away for a long time. Nicole was with me when I really needed her.

"I have to tell you everything you missed," she says. "You wouldn't *believe* how much happened in the first two days of eighth grade. But don't worry. I'll catch you up on *everything*."

Mom gets outta the car and comes around to the sidewalk. She closes my door and then hugs Nicole. "Okay, girls," she says, "I'll see you back at home, and I'll pick up a pizza for dinner."

"Get it from Polazzo's," Nicole says. "Anthony's working tonight. He'll make it extra good for you."

"Isn't that romantic?" I say in my most singsongy voice. I even clutch my heart and pretend to swoon. "Anthony has to be the best boyfriend in the whole wide world!"

"Oh my God!" Nicole covers her face. "How long are you gonna do this?"

"Um, forever," I tell her. "I thought you knew that." We both laugh.

Mom laughs, too, and goes back around to the driver's side of the car. Before she gets in, she says, "Come straight home after Woman Group."

Me and Nicole's sleepovers are on Saturdays, but since we missed last week, we decided to double up this week. Today at my house. Tomorrow at hers. Just to get us back on track. We only have one more year of weekly sleepovers, and I don't wanna miss any of them.

Ayla and Gina finally catch up to us, and I wave to them. Gina waves back, and even Ayla gives me a smile. Maybe she's happy to see me, too.

We all walk up the path to the Center, Nicole talking the whole way. "We're in the same class for earth science and English, which is good because I need you to tell me what those books are about. Like the foreshadowing and all that. Oh yeah, we have to read *Born a Crime*. I got a copy for you so you can start reading." She's talking so fast, I don't think I'll ever get a word in. "And we have the same lunch, too, which is the most important thing, of course."

I get it. I know what she's doing.

So when we get near the Center's front doors, after Gina and Ayla go inside, I put my arm on Nicole's and say, "Wait a minute."

She stops walking and turns to look at me. "What? Are you—?"

"I'm okay," I say quietly. "Really. I'm okay."

And it's kinda true. I *am* okay.

I mean, it's been hard. Really, *really* hard. And I know things aren't gonna get easier right away. But standing out here, right now, I'm definitely okay.

"Did I tell you how glad I am that you're staying?" she asks. "I mean, I know it's only because of everything that happened, but—"

"And because of you."

We hug again, quicker this time. Then Nicole says, "Come on. We can't be late for Woman Group. You're the one who dragged us into this thing!"

"*Dragged?*"

"You know what I mean!"

She literally pulls me into the Center. Inside, with the little kids running around and the noise and the boys jumping over piles of their backpacks and everything happening all at the same time, this is exactly what I need.

I almost gave all of this up.

"You ready?" she asks me, still looking at me like I could break.

I nod. "Ready."

I take a deep breath and we walk down the hall together. Like we've done a million times before.

memories, part two

some memories
hurt so much
they make you want
to run away

that's what i do
i run away
from memories
from feelings

but not this time

this time i will stay
and remember
and feel
until i'm strong
and confident
and whole

RESOURCES

• • • • • • •

As Caprice discovers, it is important for survivors of abuse to find someone to talk to about what has happened or is happening to them. For Caprice, this involves talking to Nicole and then to her parents about what her uncle did. Those are the people she trusts to confide in. When Nicole doesn't know how to help Caprice, she turns to her own mother—another form of getting support.

Other people survivors can talk to might be a therapist, a guidance counselor, a trusted teacher, or a sibling. In some cases, they might feel more comfortable talking to someone who is not already a part of their life. RAINN, the nation's largest anti-sexual violence organization, runs the National Sexual Assault Hotline at 1-800-656-HOPE (1-800-656-4673), which is a free call and is open 24 hours a day, 7 days a week. You can also live chat with trained professionals on RAINN's website, RAINN.org.

Whatever you have been through or are going through, know that you are not alone.

ACKNOWLEDGMENTS

• • • • • •

Thanks to my wonderful family: Mom, Lisa, Rashid, Denise, Mike, Haadiyah, Angela, Mordecai, Alyssa, Hamza, Hasan, and Halima. C'mon, y'all know I couldn't do any of this without you!

And many thanks to Rita Williams-Garcia, Tamara Branch, Mark Broomfield, Leslie Margolis, Emily Jenkins, Elizabeth Eulberg, Caron Levis, and Aviva Cashmira Kakar for all your help and encouragement, especially with *this* book!

And, of course, thanks to David Levithan for understanding how important this book was to me and giving me the time and space I needed to write it.

ABOUT THE AUTHOR

· · · · · · ·

Coe Booth is the award-winning author of *Kinda Like Brothers* (a book set in the same community as *Caprice*) and the YA novels *Tyrell*, *Kendra*, and *Bronxwood*. Before becoming a writer, she worked with teenagers and families in crisis, including victims of child abuse and neglect.

Coe was born in the Bronx and still lives in the Bronx, with occasional detours to live in places like Paris. You can find out more about her and her books at coebooth.com.